Very Bad Momentum A gripping high-stakes Techno-thriller full of Conspiracy, Politics, Technology, Action and Espionage

Marcelo Palacios

Published by INDEPENDENT PUBLISHER, 2024.

This is a work of fiction. Similarities to real people, places, or events are entirely coincidental.

VERY BAD MOMENTUM A GRIPPING HIGH-STAKES TECHNO-THRILLER FULL OF CONSPIRACY,POLITICS,TECHNOLOGY,ACTION AND ESPIONAGE

First edition. November 20, 2024.

Copyright © 2024 Marcelo Palacios.

ISBN: 979-8230265146

Written by Marcelo Palacios.

Also by Marcelo Palacios

El Club de los Pecados Un Thriller Psicológico
La Habitación Resonante Un Thriller Psicológico
Mentiras en Código Un Thriller Político
The Political Lies A Political Thriller
Sin's Fraternity A Psychological Thriller
El Cuarto de los Ecos Un Thriller Psicologico lleno de Suspenso
The Room of Echoes A Psychological Thriller Full of Suspense
El Espejo Perturbador Un Thriller Psicologico
The Disturbing Mirror A Psychological Thriller
Luces Apagadas en la Ciudad Brillante Un Thriller Psicológico,Crimen y Policial
Lights Out in the Shining City A Psychological, Crime and Police Thriller
Under the Cloak of Horror A Criminal Psychological Thriller full of Abuse, Corruption, Mystery, Suspense and Adventure
The Housemaid's Shadow A Psychological Thriller
Unraveling Marriage, Unraveling Divorce A Domestic Thriller
Broadband Horizons : A Technothriller Cyberpunk-Steampunk Novel
Mindstorm Protocol Expansion : A Post-Apocalyptic, Dystopian and Technological Thriller Science Fiction Novel
The Power of Invisible Chains : A Conspiracy, Crime & Political Thriller
The Watcher's Silent Crusade : A Police Procedurals & Crime Thriller
Very Bad Momentum A gripping high-stakes Techno-thriller full of Conspiracy,Politics,Technology,Action and Espionage

Table of Contents

Chapter 1: THE MISSION 1
Chapter 2: First Look at the Club 3
Chapter 3: The First Murder 6
Chapter 4: Secrets Revealed 9
Chapter 5: The Quest for the Secret 12
Chapter 6: The Shadows of the Past 15
Chapter 7: Unexpected Revelations 18
Chapter 8: In the Web of Deception 22
Chapter 9: The Money Trail 25
Chapter 10: The Enigma of Contacts 29
Chapter 11: The Network of Víctor Morales 32
Chapter 12: The Interview with Carla Núñez 35
Chapter 13: The Shadow of Truth 37
Chapter 14: The Closed Door 40
Chapter 15: The Shadow of the Informant 42
Chapter 16: The Hidden Connection 45
Chapter 17: The Secrets of Global Consult 48
Chapter 18: The Shadow of Antonio Ruiz 51
Chapter 19: Revelations in the Country House 54
Chapter 20: The Confrontation 56
Chapter 21: The Fissures in the Net 59
Chapter 22: The Double Life of Elena Martinez 62
Chapter 23: The Final Confrontation 64
Chapter 24: Elena's Revelations 67
Chapter 25: The Plan in Motion 70
Chapter 26: The Confession of Antonio Ruiz 72
Chapter 27: The Discovery at Francisco Delgado's Residence 74
Chapter 28: The Trial of the Responsible 76
Chapter 29: The Repercussions on the Business World 78
Chapter 30: The Last Traps of the Net 80
Chapter 31: The Network Dismantled 82
Chapter 32: New Threats 84
Chapter 33: The Labyrinth of Truth 86

Chapter 34: In the Eye of the Hurricane 88
Chapter 35: The Final Revelation 90
Chapter 36: Echoes of the Past.. 92
Chapter 37: The Confrontation... 94
Chapter 38: The Last Game 96
Chapter 39: The Deadly Game.. 98
Chapter 40: New Horizons.. 100

Chapter 1: THE MISSION

Lucas Ferrer was in his office, a gloomy place located in the most run-down part of the city. Afternoon light filtered through the dusty blinds, casting jagged shadows on the walls. The air was permeated with the smell of cigarettes and whiskey, which mixed with the humidity of an impending storm looming on the horizon. As he watched the first drops begin to hit the glass, the sharp ringing of his phone broke the silence.

On the other end of the line, a deep, authoritative male voice made him an offer he couldn't refuse. There were no names, only one proposal: a million dollars to infiltrate one of the city's most exclusive circles, the Sin Club, to uncover the truth behind a series of disappearances. The victims were all young women, with no apparent connections to each other, but clues pointed to the club being the common link.

Lucas accepted without hesitation. He knew that while money was tempting, it was the challenge that really drew him in. After years in the business, simple cases no longer provided him with the same adrenaline rush as before. And something about the way the voice had described the club—with its air of mystery and decay—gave him a sense of unease, one that drove him to want to know more.

After hanging up the phone, Lucas lit a cigarette and stared at the rain, allowing the smoke to rise in lazy spirals. A million dollars... but also a very high risk. The Sin Club was known for its luxuries and its shadows, a place where the city's richest and most powerful satiated their darkest desires. No one, outside of the members, knew what was really going on within its walls.

Curiosity overcame caution. It didn't take long for him to move. He rummaged through his desk until he found the folder containing what little information he had gathered about the club in the past: a list of names that meant nothing to him, some blurry photos, and an address in the most exclusive part of town. Lucas knew he would need more than that to infiltrate.

An hour later, he was in his car, driving into the city center. The rain was falling harder, creating a monotonous rhythm on the roof of the vehicle. As the windshield wiper swept through the water, his mind began to process what he knew. The Sin Club was not only a place of leisure for the wealthiest, it was also a kind of refuge for those who wanted to hide something.

I knew that the first part of the job would be simple: enter the club and pretend to be a new member interested in the "services" they offered. From there, everything would depend on his ability to blend in and gain the trust of those pulling the strings.

When he arrived at his destination, the club's lights were shining brightly through the curtain of rain. A valet took the keys to his car without asking questions, and Lucas walked toward the driveway. The building had an imposing, elegant façade, but something about the way the structure stood among the others gave it a sense of isolation. It was as if it was designed so that the outside world would not have access to what was happening inside.

As you walked through the doors, the club's interior revealed itself as an opulent space, decorated with marble, velvet and gold reflecting the light of gigantic chandeliers. The soft music created a sensual atmosphere, and the furtive glances of the attendees suggested that everyone was keeping secrets.

Lucas was greeted by a man who introduced himself as **Luis**, one of those in charge of managing access to new members. Luis took him to a private room, where he was offered a whiskey while his credentials were reviewed. Luke had created a false identity weeks before, foreseeing that this day would come. When Luis returned, with a smile on his lips, he handed him a black card with his fake name engraved in gold. "Welcome to Sin Club," he said with a look that hid more than it revealed.

With the card in hand, Lucas felt that he had just crossed a line from which he might not be able to return. But that wouldn't stop him. It had a clear objective: to uncover what was hidden under the mask of luxury and decadence. He knew that the missing had left a faint trail, but if anyone could follow him to the end, it was him.

He rose, gritting his teeth. The real work had just begun.

Chapter 2: First Look at the Club

The interior of the Sin Club was imbued with an air of decadent opulence. The walls were adorned with dark wood paneling and crimson velvet tapestries, while crystal chandeliers cast golden reflections on the polished marble floor. Soft, almost hypnotic music filled the space, mingling with the laughter and murmurs of the attendees. Lucas Ferrer, with his new identity as **Eduardo Sánchez**, moved among the members of the club, trying not to attract attention while absorbing every detail of his surroundings.

Luis, the person in charge of his access, led him through a large and elegant hall, to a room where a private party was being held. As he approached, Lucas noticed the presence of prominent figures of high society: politicians, businessmen and celebrities, all with enigmatic faces and calculating looks. Women dressed with dazzling elegance, and men wore tailored suits that seemed almost defiant in their sophistication.

As he entered the room, Lucas felt the weight of curious glances, as if everyone present were assessing his value. Luis said goodbye with a formal gesture and got lost in the crowd, leaving him at the mercy of the atmosphere full of sensuality and secrets. Lucas decided that the best way to blend in was to act confident, as if he really belonged in that environment.

As he moved around the room, he looked around carefully. The subtlest details were the most revealing: the whispers between select groups, the fleeting touches of contact that seemed more meaningful than they should be, and the gestures of complicity that betrayed hidden relationships. It was evident that Sin Club not only offered an escape from everyday life, but also a web of complex and often corrupt connections.

In a corner of the room, Lucas noticed a woman who immediately captured his attention. She wore a tight black dress that enhanced her figure and her blonde hair, gathered in an elegant bun, stood out against the contrast against the dark background. She was in conversation with an older, imposing-looking man. The woman seemed aloof and reserved, but there was something about her posture and the way she looked around that suggested she was more involved in the situation than she appeared.

4

Lucas approached one of the cocktail tables and took a glass of champagne, while his eyes followed the woman's figure. The conversation she had with the man was whispering, and the tone was too low to capture details. However, Lucas captured fragments of the conversation that alluded to the possibility of an imminent operation within the club.

Just then, a man approached Lucas, offering him a polite smile. "First time here, friend?" he asked in a foreign accent. "My name is **Marcelo**. It's always interesting to see new faces this holiday season."

Lucas, adopting a relaxed tone, replied. "Yes, it's my first time. I'm here for business reasons. I've been told a lot about this place."

Marcelo nodded with a sympathetic smile. "Of course, we all have our reasons. If you need information or just someone to chat with, don't hesitate to give me a call." Marcelo handed him a card with his name and phone number before walking away.

Lucas put the card in his pocket, knowing that any connection he could make in that environment could be valuable. However, the real surprise came when he noticed that the woman in the black dress was watching him. Their eyes met briefly before she looked away, a gesture Lucas interpreted as an invitation or a warning.

He decided to approach her, maintaining a casual and friendly tone. "Hello, it looks like this is your first time too," he said, trying to start a conversation. The woman looked at him with a mixture of surprise and distrust, but then allowed the conversation to flow.

"I'm **Valeria Montes**," she said, introducing herself in a soft, calculated voice. "And yes, this is my first time here. What brings you to this place?"

Lucas, maintaining his façade, responded. "I'm here to learn more about the club. I've heard it's the perfect place to make high-level contacts."

Valeria raised an eyebrow, clearly intrigued but cautious. "And what kind of contacts are you looking for?"

Before I could answer, a tall, well-dressed man interrupted the conversation. "Valeria, is everything okay?" he asked in a protective, almost possessive tone. Valeria nodded and turned to Lucas. "I apologize, but it seems that I have to attend to this guest. It's been a pleasure to meet you, Eduardo."

With one last enigmatic look, Valeria walked away along with the man. Lucas stared at her, wondering if her presence at the club was just a coincidence or if there was more to her than it seemed.

As Lucas continued to explore the club, his mind was filled with unanswered questions. What secrets were these socialites hiding? And what role did Valeria play in all this? He knew he had to stay alert and cunning if he wanted to uncover the truth behind the disappearances and the dark world of Sin Club.

Chapter 3: The First Murder

The night at the Sin Club continued its course with an atmosphere full of sensuality and secrets. Lucas Ferrer, still adapting to the exclusive environment of the place, decided that it was time to move to less crowded areas, where he could observe without attracting attention. Soft music and dim lights created an environment that seemed designed to hide both pleasures and crimes.

Lucas had managed to establish a certain familiarity with some of the attendees, thanks to his ability to blend in with high society. He moved between conversations and laughter, trying to capture any relevant detail. However, his investigation was interrupted by an unexpected event that would change the course of the night.

In the middle of a conversation with Marcelo, the foreign-accented man he had previously met, Lucas noticed a growing murmur in the main room. Guests began to congregate around a focal point, their expressions mixing surprise and fear. Lucas approached, feigning curiosity, and found the source of the commotion in the center of the circle.

A young woman, whom Lucas had seen earlier in the club, lay on the ground, motionless. Her white dress was stained with blood, and the scene was a chaos of anguished screams and whispers. The body was surrounded by a group of people who were trying to revive her, but it was evident that there was no hope. Lucas felt a knot in his stomach when he realized that the woman was none other than **Andrea**, one of the missing women he had mentioned in his initial investigation.

Marcelo approached Lucas, his face pale. "This is a nightmare," he murmured. "I never thought something like this could happen here."

Lucas observed the place carefully, noticing the reaction of the other members. Some seemed genuinely affected, while others kept a prudent distance, as if the chaos did not touch them at all. The atmosphere in the room changed drastically; What had been a celebration full of luxury and hedonism now turned into a scene of horror.

The police arrived quickly, disrupting the club's activities and beginning to secure the area. Lucas stood in the shadows, watching as officers took notes and asked questions. His main goal was not to be identified, while he tried to gather any information that might be useful for his research.

As detectives focused on the crime scene, Lucas approached a group of club employees who were visibly agitated. One of them, a young man in an impeccable uniform, looked particularly nervous. Lucas approached and asked him a casual question about what had happened.

"I'm sorry, sir, but I can't talk about this," the young man said, his voice trembling. "This is a disaster. No one knows who could have done something like that."

Lucas continued his exploration, looking for any clues that might indicate how the murder had been carried out. He noticed that the club's security had increased, with more guards on patrol and staff members being interrogated. The fact that a member of the club had been killed in the middle of the event meant that the situation was extremely serious.

Suddenly, as Lucas examined the area around the body, he found something that caught his attention: a small fragment of black cloth that looked like it had been torn in the fight. He carefully picked it up and put it in his pocket, hoping it could be a crucial clue in the case.

Later, while Lucas was in the lobby, he saw Valeria Montes talking to one of the detectives. She looked frustrated and nervous, looking around anxiously. Lucas approached discreetly, trying to listen to their conversation.

"It's crazy," Valeria said, her voice filled with despair. "How is it possible that someone came in and did this without anyone noticing?"

The detective looked at her with a mixture of understanding and skepticism. "We are doing everything we can to resolve this. If you have any relevant information, you should let us know."

Valeria nodded and, apparently defeated, walked away with her eyes fixed on the ground. Lucas decided to approach her, wanting to know if he could get any additional information or at least clear up his own doubts.

"Hello, Valeria," Lucas said, approaching with a friendly smile. "It looks like tonight has been more complicated than we expected."

Valeria looked at him with surprise, as if she hadn't noticed his presence until that moment. "Yes, it has been... unexpected. Are you also here for the murder?"

Lucas nodded, trying to maintain a casual attitude. "Yes, I'm trying to understand what could have led to this. I can't stop thinking about what it means to all of us."

Valeria sighed. "Everyone here has secrets, and I'm not sure how much we can trust those around us. But if you're interested, we might try to find out more about what's going on. Maybe it's not a coincidence."

Lucas offered her an approving smile. "I agree. What happened tonight is just the tip of the iceberg. We're going to need all the help we can get to find out the truth."

As the police continued their investigation and club members tried to get back to normal, Lucas retreated to a corner, watching the scene with a mixture of trepidation and determination. The night had begun with a simple assignment, but now, with Andrea's death, the situation had become much more complex and dangerous.

Chapter 4: Secrets Revealed

The next morning, news of the murder at the Sin Club had shaken the city. The media was full of speculation and theories about what had happened, while the police continued with the investigation. Lucas Ferrer, with his identity of **Eduardo Sánchez** still intact, decided that it was time to delve into the mystery that had begun the night before.

He woke up in his small apartment, his mind entangled in the events of the previous night. The fragment of black cloth he had found at the scene of the crime was still in his pocket, and Lucas knew he had to examine it in more detail. The clue was subtle, but in his experience, any clue, no matter how small, could be crucial to solving the case.

After a quick and reluctant breakfast, Lucas went to his office. The small office was full of cluttered files, old photographs, and documents about previous cases. He placed the piece of cloth under a magnifying glass and began to examine it. The fabric was of high quality, with a pattern that looked sophisticated and expensive, indicating that it probably belonged in a luxury garment.

As Lucas analyzed the fragment, his mind kept returning to the conversation with Valeria Montes. The woman seemed to be as confused and affected as he was, but her behavior had been enigmatic. He decided he needed more information about her, so he started researching her background. He used his contacts and skills to discover that Valeria was a well-known figure in the world of high society, known for her work in charities and her connections to politicians and businessmen.

Lucas discovered that Valeria had been one of the founders of a charity that allegedly supported victims of domestic violence. However, there were rumors that the organization was embroiled in controversies and allegations of mismanagement of funds. This information could be useful, considering that Andrea, the victim, had been a young woman who could have been involved in social causes.

With a new goal in mind, Lucas decided to return to the Sin Club to take a close look at Valeria and see if he could uncover any connection between her and the murder. The club had been temporarily closed for investigation, but

Lucas had access thanks to his new identity. Upon entering, he noticed that the place was deserted, with a sense of desolation that contrasted with the nightlife he had experienced.

Lucas went to the club's security office, where he met **Luis**, the manager who had introduced him the night before. Luis was working hard to restore order, but Lucas could see the tension on his face.

"Good morning, Luis," Lucas said with a gentle smile. "How's everything going after last night's incident?"

Luis looked at him with a mixture of frustration and resignation. "It's chaos, Eduardo. We are trying to cooperate with the police, but the club is at the center of a media whirlwind. It's impossible to stay calm when the media is trampling on everything."

Lucas nodded in understanding. "It must be difficult. I just wanted to see if I could help in some way, maybe with information that might be relevant to the investigation."

Luis looked at him in surprise, but then seemed to consider the offer. "Well, any help is welcome. If you find anything, let us know. The truth is that we are all worried. Andrea was not just a customer, she also had a significant influence on our operations."

Lucas decided it was time to dig deeper. While Luis was busy, Lucas went to the room where the murder had taken place. Even though the scene had been cleaned up, Lucas noticed that some objects were still out of place. He approached a corner of the room where he had seen Andrea's body and began to look for more clues.

In a hidden corner, he found a small crumpled note under a rug. He took it and unrolled it carefully. The note contained a cryptic message: "Time is ticking. Find the secret before it's too late."

Lucas put the note away along with the piece of cloth, his mind full of questions. What secret was hidden in the club? And what connection did he have with Andrea's murder? He decided that he should go back to find Valeria to interrogate her more directly. The information he had found about his charity could provide an important link in the investigation.

Later that day, Lucas managed to track down Valeria in one of the charity's offices. He found her sitting at her desk, surrounded by papers and with a tired expression. Valeria looked up when she saw him enter, her face showing a mixture of surprise and caution.

"Eduardo?" asked Valeria, trying to sound surprised. "What are you doing here?"

Lucas approached with a professional smile. "I just wanted to talk to you about what happened last night. I'm interested in better understanding the context and any information you may have about Andrea. I'm really trying to help solve the case."

Valeria looked at him with a mixture of skepticism and hope. "I'm sorry, Eduardo. It is a difficult time for everyone. What I can tell you might not be much, but if you're really here to help, I'm willing to listen to what's on your mind."

Valeria led him to a meeting room, where she began to talk in more detail about her work in the organization. Luke listened attentively, analyzing every word and every gesture. As the conversation progressed, Valeria began to relax a bit, allowing Lucas to pick up on details that might be relevant to his investigation.

Valeria mentioned that Andrea had been involved in several projects to support women in vulnerable situations, but that she had begun to show strange behavior in the weeks leading up to her death. "She was worried about something, but she never told me exactly what it was," Valeria admitted. "He said he had found something that could affect a lot of people."

Lucas nodded, making a mental note. "I understand. If you discover anything else, please let me know. I'm sure that any detail, no matter how small, can be crucial."

As he said goodbye, Lucas felt like he was starting to put the pieces of the puzzle together. The club, Valeria, the charity, and Andrea's murder formed a complex enigma, but each new clue brought him one step closer to the truth.

Chapter 5: The Quest for the Secret

With night falling on the city, Lucas Ferrer was in his apartment, reviewing the notes and clues he had collected during the day. The small cryptic note and the fragment of black cloth were the main pieces of an increasingly intricate puzzle. Lucas was determined to uncover the truth behind Andrea's murder and the mysterious message he had found.

The note, with its enigmatic message about "finding the secret before it's too late," kept him on the edge of his seat. I knew I had to dig deeper into the connections between the club, Valeria's charity, and the other characters involved. The question on his mind was: what secret was hidden and how was it related to Andrea's death?

He decided it was time to further investigate the charity Valeria was involved in. He had mentioned that Andrea was worried about something related to the organization, and that could be the key to solving the case. With a list of contacts and addresses, Lucas began his search.

The first stop was the charity's headquarters, a stylish office building in the city centre. The office was modern, with a sober but elegant décor. Lucas introduced himself at the reception desk, explaining that he was there to ask some questions about Andrea and the organization's recent projects.

The receptionist looked at him curiously. "I'm sorry, sir, but you'll need an appointment to talk to someone about those issues. We cannot provide information without proper authorization."

Lucas smiled kindly. "I understand. However, my interest is in helping to solve Andrea's case. Maybe I could talk to someone who is familiar with his latest projects."

After a brief discussion, the receptionist agreed to contact **Beatriz**, one of the people in charge of the organization, to talk to Lucas. Beatriz was a middle-aged woman, with a gentle but professional expression. He received her in his office, where Lucas began to inquire about recent projects.

"Andrea was a very dedicated volunteer," Beatriz said as she reviewed some documents. "I was involved in several projects to support women and children at risk. I remember that in the last few weeks I was especially worried. He mentioned that he had discovered something that could compromise the organization, but he did not give me clear details."

Lucas listened attentively. "Do you know if Andrea shared this information with anyone else? Or if there were some recent problems in the organization that might have affected it?"

Beatriz frowned. "I'm not sure. Andrea had access to confidential information because of her position, and although she didn't usually talk much about her concerns, I think there was something that made her uneasy. If you want, you can review their files. Maybe you'll find something useful."

Lucas thanked the offer and went into the office archive area. He went through documents related to Andrea's projects and found reports and correspondence that seemed harmless at first. However, upon closer examination, he noticed some emails that mentioned an internal audit and possible irregularities in the handling of funds.

While Lucas was investigating, he received a call from his contact at the police, **Detective Sanchez**. "Hello, Eduardo. We wanted to inform you that we have found some additional clues at the scene of the crime. It appears that Andrea had a mobile phone with suspicious call logs and messages. We want you to help us review the data."

Lucas accepted the request and went to the police station to check the mobile phone. Detective Sanchez handed him the device, along with a copy of the call and message logs. Lucas examined the phone, looking for any relevant information that could connect the murder to recent events at the charity.

In the records, she found several messages from an unknown number who appeared to have been in frequent contact with Andrea. The messages were short and enigmatic, with one containing a warning: "Be careful what you discover. Some truths are darker than you imagine."

Lucas wondered if this unknown number was related to the murder or if it was part of a larger game. He decided to track down the number, and discovered that it was registered in the name of **Alberto Ramírez**, a name he had not found in his previous investigation. Alberto was a well-known businessman with connections in politics and organized crime.

Lucas realized that he needed to find out more about Alberto Ramírez. So he decided to go to his office, located in an elegant skyscraper in the city's business district. Upon arrival, he found the security of the building and asked to speak with Alberto under the pretext of a routine investigation.

After waiting in the reception room, he was finally ushered to Alberto's office. The businessman was a middle-aged man with an imposing presence. Seeing Lucas enter, he showed a calculating smile.

"How can I help you?" asked Alberto, with a look that seemed to read Lucas accurately.

Lucas remained professional. "I'm investigating Andrea's murder and I found your number on her phone. I'd like to ask you a few questions about your relationship with her."

Alberto's expression hardened, but he remained calm. "I'm not sure what I might know about that. My relationship with Andrea was purely professional."

Lucas continued with the interview, trying to unravel any information that might be useful. Alberto was evasive, but Lucas noticed that there was something in his behavior that didn't fit. The businessman seemed to be hiding something, and Lucas was determined to find out what it was.

After the conversation with Alberto, Lucas returned to his apartment, exhausted but determined. He had found several pieces of a puzzle, but the full picture was still far from clear. The secret mentioned in the note and the links between Andrea, the charity and Alberto Ramírez remained a tangle of uncertainty.

Lucas knew he had to keep investigating, looking for any connections that might unravel the mystery behind Andrea's death. As the sun set, he prepared his mind for a new day full of enigmas and secrets to discover.

Chapter 6: The Shadows of the Past

Lucas Ferrer woke up early the next day, determined to continue unraveling the mystery of Andrea's murder. The information obtained so far had been revealing, but there were still many pieces to be placed in the puzzle. The encounter with Alberto Ramírez had left him with a sense of unease, and he knew that he had to delve deeper into his past to understand his connection to the case.

He began his day by reviewing documents and emails related to the charity. The information about the internal audit was especially relevant, and Lucas decided that he should investigate whether there were any hidden documents or reports that could give more clues about the aforementioned irregularities.

Upon leaving his apartment, Lucas headed to a public library, seeking access to business records and public archives that might shed light on Alberto Ramirez and his businesses. I knew the businessman had a complicated history, but I didn't have all the details. Upon arriving at the library, he headed to the business records section and began looking for information about the companies associated with Alberto.

After hours of investigation, Lucas uncovered several front companies and connections to suspicious activity. One of the companies, **Grupo Ramirez**, had several contracts with charities and appeared to be linked to the money Andrea had been investigating. Financial reports showed suspicious transfers and contracts with unknown companies, suggesting a possible money laundering scheme.

As Lucas was reviewing the documents, he received an unexpected text message. It was from Valeria Montes, who asked him to meet her at a nearby café. The invitation came as a surprise, but Lucas decided that he should accept the opportunity to get more information.

At the café, Valeria was sitting at a table in the back, looking nervously around. Seeing Lucas, she stood up and greeted him with a mixture of relief and anxiety.

"Hello, Eduardo. Thank you for coming," Valeria said as she sat down. "There's something I need to talk to you about. I've been thinking a lot about Andrea and what could have happened to her."

Lucas sat down in front of her, watching her worried expression. "What have you discovered?"

Valeria sighed. "I've been going through Andrea's files and emails, and I found something that might be relevant. It appears that she was investigating certain donations and contracts at the charity that did not match the official reports. I think he may have found something important before his death."

Lucas leaned forward, interested. "Do you have access to those documents? They could be key to understanding what was really happening."

Valeria nodded and took a folder out of her bag. He opened it and showed Lucas several documents and emails that revealed inconsistencies in the organization's donations and expenses. Among the documents, Lucas found a series of communications between Andrea and an unknown contact that appeared to be related to the suspicious transfers.

"This contact," Valeria said, pointing to a name in the emails, "appears in several Andrea documents. I couldn't find much information about him, but it seems that he was involved in questionable donations."

Lucas took note of the name and decided to investigate further. The conversation with Valeria had given him a new direction in his investigation, and he was sure that he should delve deeper into the contact mentioned in the documents.

After the meeting with Valeria, Lucas went to Grupo **Ramírez**'s headquarters to get more information about the unknown contact. Upon arrival, he was met with a modern and luxurious office, with a reception that seemed to be the center of operations of a high-profile company.

Lucas showed up at the front desk and asked to speak to someone who could provide him with information about the company's contracts and donations. After a few minutes of waiting, he was ushered into the office of **Ricardo Gomez**, a high-level executive at the company.

Ricardo was a man of confident appearance, with an air of authority that was evident in his behavior. Upon receiving Lucas, he showed a professional but cold smile.

"Hello, Mr. Gomez. I'm Eduardo Sanchez, and I'm investigating some irregularities in donations and contracts related to your company. Could you provide me with information about recent contacts and transactions?"

Ricardo looked at him with a mixture of curiosity and distrust. "Irregularities? I'm not sure what you mean. All of our reports are in order."

Lucas remained calm. "I have found some documents that suggest otherwise. I would like to review any additional information they may have."

Ricardo frowned, but agreed to show some additional reports. As Lucas reviewed the documents, he noticed that there were several transactions and contracts that matched those found in Andrea's emails. However, upon examining the documents more closely, he noticed that some of the names and details had been altered or removed.

"It seems that there is something that is not entirely clear," Lucas said, trying not to reveal his suspicion. "Could you explain to me why some of these documents appear to be incomplete or modified?"

Ricardo looked uncomfortable, but tried to keep his composure. "Our audit department handles all the documents. If there are any problems, you should talk to them."

Lucas decided it was time to end the conversation. "Thank you for your time, Mr. Gomez. I will continue to investigate and if I find anything else, I will get in touch."

With the documents in hand and new clues about the unknown contact, Lucas returned to his apartment to analyze the information. The connection between the charity's donations and **Grupo Ramirez** seemed clearer, but the role of the unknown contact remained a mystery.

That night, as Lucas was going through the documents and trying to connect the dots, he received an unexpected call from Valeria. "Eduardo, I need to talk to you urgently. There's something that I just discovered and I think it could be crucial to the case."

Lucas accepted the invitation and went to Valeria's office. The mystery of Andrea's murder was taking an increasingly dark turn, and it was clear that the pieces of the puzzle were starting to fall into place.

Chapter 7: Unexpected Revelations

Night had fallen with a blanket of mystery that seemed to envelop the city. Lucas Ferrer, after Valeria's urgent call, went to the charity's office. The tension in the air was palpable, and Lucas felt like he was about to discover something crucial to solving Andrea's murder.

When he arrived at the office, Valeria was waiting for him at the entrance, with an expression that showed a mixture of anxiety and determination. "Thank you for coming so quickly, Eduardo. I couldn't wait to share this with you."

Lucas followed Valeria into her office, where she pulled a file from her desk and spread it out to him. "While going through some additional documents, I found something very interesting. This file contains records of communications and transactions that were not in the previous reports."

Lucas opened the file carefully and began to examine the documents. Among them, he found a series of emails that spoke of a significant transaction and an agreement with a security company. The company appeared to be involved in protecting sensitive data, but the contract was full of loopholes and omissions.

Valeria leaned forward, her voice low and urgent. "These documents suggest that Andrea had found something that could compromise the organization. She was investigating possible internal corruption, and it appears that the data was being manipulated to cover up irregularities."

Lucas nodded, observing the details. "This is very revealing. It seems that Andrea was on the right track in discovering these problems. Do you know who was behind the security company or if anyone in the organization might be involved in the cover-up?"

Valeria shook her head. "I don't have all the information, but I've heard rumors about a former employee who might be connected to the security company. His name is **Tomas Fernandez**, and he is said to have been involved in questionable practices before leaving the organization."

With a new goal in mind, Lucas decided that he had to find Tomás Fernández. "Thank you for your help, Valeria. I'll investigate Tomas Fernandez and see what I can discover. If you find anything else, please let me know."

Lucas left Valeria's office with a sense of determination. The mystery of Andrea's murder was taking shape, and each new clue brought him closer to the truth. He decided that he should begin investigating Tomás Fernández immediately.

His first stop was an old address that Valeria had told him about. The address belonged to an apartment in a residential complex on the outskirts of the city. Upon arriving, Lucas found a dilapidated building that seemed to have seen better days. She went upstairs to Tomás's apartment and knocked on the door.

After a few moments, the door opened and Lucas came face to face with Tomas Fernandez. He was a man in his 40s, with an expression of surprise that quickly turned to caution at the sight of Lucas.

"Yes?" asked Tomás with a tone that reflected a mixture of distrust and curiosity.

"Hello, Tomás. I'm Eduardo Sánchez, a private investigator. I am investigating Andrea's murder and have found some connections between your name and the security company that was linked to her case. I need to ask you some questions."

Thomas frowned and looked at Lucas suspiciously. "I'm not sure what you have in mind. I have nothing to do with it."

Lucas decided to be direct. "I have information that suggests you were involved in the security company and data manipulation. What can you tell me about that?"

Thomas looked uncomfortable, but he tried to keep his composure. "Look, what we did at the security company was nothing more than normal work. Those accusations are exaggerated."

Lucas was not fooled. "I have found documents that suggest otherwise. It seems that you were involved in questionable practices and that you might know something about what Andrea was investigating."

Thomas sighed and, after a moment's hesitation, sat down in a worn-out armchair. "It's okay. I may have been involved in some shady dealings, but I have nothing to do with Andrea's murder. She was investigating something she shouldn't have touched, but I don't know exactly what it was."

Luke leaned forward, his interest aroused by Thomas's words. "Do you know who else might be involved? Is there anything you can tell me about the people who were behind the security company?"

Tomás looked at him with concern. "There is a name you should investigate: **Raúl Mendoza**. He was the head of the security company and he was up to his neck in all this. If anyone knows anything about Andrea's murder, it's probably him."

With this new information, Lucas said goodbye to Tomás and went to Raúl Mendoza's office. He knew he had to act fast before any clues faded away. The truth behind Andrea's murder was getting closer and closer, and Lucas was determined to uncover all the secrets that had been hidden.

Arriving at Raul Mendoza's office, Lucas was met with a sleek, modern building, which seemed to reflect the status and wealth of the man he was about to interview. He entered the reception and asked to speak to Raúl. The receptionist, hearing Lucas' name, led him to a private office on the top floor of the building.

Raul Mendoza was a middle-aged man with an air of unflappable confidence. When he received Lucas, his smile was a mixture of cordiality and disdain. "Hello, Eduardo. How can I help you?"

Lucas stood his ground. "I am investigating Andrea's murder and have found some connections between your company and the case. I need to ask you some questions about your relationship with her and your company."

Raul looked at him with interest and a hint of amusement. "I'm sorry, but I'm not sure what you might be looking for. My company follows all the regulations and we have never been in trouble with the law."

Lucas decided to be direct. "I have found documents that suggest that your company was involved in questionable activities and that Andrea was investigating wrongdoing. What can you tell me about it?"

Raul remained calm, but his eyes showed a spark of nervousness. "I have no idea what Andrea may have found. My company is responsible for providing security and protection. If there was a problem, I wasn't aware of it."

Lucas said goodbye to Raúl, feeling that he had touched a nerve. The truth about Andrea's murder was slowly emerging, and each interview revealed new layers of deception and corruption. With the names of Raúl Mendoza and

Tomás Fernández on his radar, Lucas was closer to solving the case, but the road to the truth was still full of obstacles and unexpected surprises.

Chapter 8: In the Web of Deception

Lucas Ferrer returned to his apartment, exhausted but determined. The meetings with Tomas Fernandez and Raul Mendoza had added new pieces to the puzzle of Andrea's murder, but they had also raised more questions. He knew he had to dig deeper into the connection between the security company and the assassination to unravel the truth.

That night, while reviewing his notes and documents, he received an anonymous email. The message contained an attachment titled "Crucial Information." The content of the email did not include text, only a link to a compressed file. Lucas was cautious but also intrigued. He decided to open the file, which contained a series of documents and emails about the security company and Grupo **Ramírez's transactions**.

Among the documents, Lucas found a series of emails that revealed a conversation between Raul Mendoza and an unknown individual, who appeared to be involved in the cover-up of wrongdoing. The conversation included mentions of cash payments and secret deals related to Andrea's investigation.

Upon examining the emails, Lucas noticed that there were references to a secret meeting in an unknown location, where details were discussed about how to handle Andrea's situation and her investigation. He also found a name that appeared repeatedly in the emails: **Roberto Salazar**, a contact of Raúl Mendoza who seemed to be in charge of the logistics of the covert operations.

With this new information, Lucas knew that he had to find Roberto Salazar. He decided to track his location and seek more details about his relationship to the case. Using research resources and contacts in the private sphere, Lucas managed to obtain an address for Roberto.

Arriving at the address provided, Lucas came across a house in a quiet, spotless-looking neighborhood. She went to the door and knocked, hoping Roberto was home. After a few moments, a woman answered the door.

"Hello, I'm Eduardo Sánchez, a private investigator. I'm looking for Roberto Salazar. Is it available?" asked Lucas.

The woman, who seemed to be Roberto's wife, looked at him in surprise. "Roberto is not home at the moment. Can I help with anything?"

Lucas was respectful but determined. "It's important that you talk to him about an investigation he's involved in. Do you know when he'll be back?"

The woman nodded. "I should be home later tonight. If you want, you can leave your phone number and I'll make sure I call you."

Lucas put down his business card and said goodbye. She knew she had to wait for Roberto to return to get answers. In the meantime, he decided to continue his investigation and visit the location of the secret meeting mentioned in the emails.

The place turned out to be an old warehouse on the outskirts of the city, a dilapidated building that had been abandoned for years. Lucas entered the warehouse, illuminated only by the light of his flashlight. The atmosphere was oppressive, and the place seemed to be filled with dust and cobwebs.

While exploring the warehouse, he found a number of documents strewn across the floor, some of which were related to the security company and undercover operations. Among the documents, Lucas discovered a contract that appeared to be a hush agreement, signed by several people, including Raul Mendoza and Roberto Salazar.

The contract contained clauses prohibiting the disclosure of information about the irregularities and cover-up of Andrea's investigation. Lucas took note of the names and dates, realizing that the contract could be a key piece in unraveling the plot behind the murder.

He returned to his apartment with the contract and documents in hand, ready to analyze them further. While he was doing so, he received an unexpected call from Roberto Salazar.

"Hello, Eduardo. I'm Roberto Salazar. I have received your message and I would like to know what this is all about. Can we talk?"

Lucas accepted the invitation and met Roberto at a discreet café in the center of the city. When they met, Roberto seemed nervous and evasive, trying to maintain a cordial attitude.

"Hello, Roberto. Thank you for meeting with me. I'm investigating Andrea's murder and I've found documents that mention you. What can you tell me about your involvement in this case?" Lucas asked, bluntly.

Roberto looked uncomfortable and looked around before answering. "Look, I don't know what you found, but I assure you that I have nothing to do with Andrea's murder. Yes, I worked for the security company and yes, I was involved in certain deals, but that doesn't mean I'm involved in his death."

Lucas looked at him with intensity. "I've seen a contract that involves you in a cover-up related to Andrea's investigation. What can you tell me about it?"

Roberto seemed to struggle with his words, but finally he spoke. "The contract is real, but I wasn't aware of all the details. My job was to coordinate certain logistical aspects, but I was not involved in the planning of the assassination."

Lucas observed the desperation in Roberto's eyes and realized that there was something more behind his words. "If you're not directly involved, who could be behind all this? Do you have any idea who might have given the order to cover up for Andrea?"

Roberto sighed, his expression of resignation showing that he knew more than he was willing to reveal. "I'm not sure about the details, but I think the key is in Raúl Mendoza. He was in command and in control of the covert operations. If anyone had a reason to eliminate Andrea, it would probably be him."

Lucas took note of the information and said goodbye to Roberto, feeling that he had made progress in the investigation. The connection between Raul Mendoza and Andrea's murder was becoming increasingly apparent, and Lucas knew he had to dig deeper into his relationship with the case.

Back at his apartment, Lucas began planning his next move. The truth about Andrea's murder was closer than ever, but there were still many questions to be answered. The path to justice was uncertain, but Lucas was determined to uncover all the hidden secrets and bring those responsible to justice.

Chapter 9: The Money Trail

Lucas Ferrer woke up early the next day, his mind full of the details of the investigation. He knew he had to act quickly to unravel the web of corruption and cover-up surrounding Andrea's case. The key piece that was missing seemed to be the flow of money involved in the cover-up operation. He decided to track the financial movements related to the security company and the Ramírez Group.

He went to the office of his private accountant, Javier, an old friend who used to help him with complicated investigations. Javier, a meticulous man with an innate knack for numbers, was willing to collaborate. "Good morning, Lucas. How can I help you today?"

Lucas sat down in front of Javier and unfolded a series of documents and emails on the table. "I am investigating a complicated case and I need to track the financial movements of the security company and the Ramírez Group. I think there could be a hidden pattern behind the transactions that may reveal something crucial."

Javier reviewed the documents carefully, frowning as he analyzed the data. "There appear to be a number of cash payments and transfers to offshore accounts. We will examine each transaction and see if we can find any irregularities."

While Javier worked on the details, Lucas decided to pay a visit to the Ramírez Group's office. I knew it was important to understand the relationship between the company and the group, and possibly find some clues that would connect the dots. Upon arrival, he found a modern, high-security building.

He showed up at the front desk and asked to speak with the CFO, **Carlos Ramírez**. The receptionist, upon verifying his identity, led him to an elegant waiting room. Lucas waited anxiously as he observed the luxurious surroundings that seemed to reflect the success and influence of the Ramírez Group.

Finally, Carlos Ramírez appeared. He was a man in his 50s, with an imposing presence and a shrewd look. "Hello, Eduardo. I've heard of you. How can I help you?"

Lucas was direct. "I am investigating Andrea's murder and have found some documents that suggest a connection between your company and the security company. I want to better understand the flow of money between the two and how they might be involved in the case."

Carlos remained calm but showed a slight tension in his expression. "My company does a lot of transactions and handles several contracts. I'm not sure what documents you're referring to, but if there's a problem, we need to solve it."

Lucas wasted no time and showed Carlos the relevant documents. "These records suggest that there are suspicious transactions that could be related to Andrea's investigation. Can you provide more information about these payments?"

Carlos reviewed the documents carefully. "It appears that some of these payments are related to security and protection contracts for special events. I don't have direct knowledge of the details, but I can provide you with more information about the contracts and accounts."

Lucas thanked Carlos for his cooperation and said goodbye, feeling that he had obtained valuable but incomplete information. While on her way to her next destination, she received a call from Javier.

"Hello, Lucas. I have reviewed the financial documents and found something interesting. There are a number of transfers to an offshore account that appears to be linked to a shell company. The money appears to have been used for cash payments and bribes."

Lucas was intrigued. "That's important. Can you trace the source of those funds and find out who's behind the account?"

Javier nodded. "I'm working on it. I'll let you know as soon as I have more details."

With this new information, Lucas decided to further investigate the shell company mentioned in the documents. The company appeared to be a front for money laundering and hiding illegal transactions. He decided to search the company's records and connections to the people involved in the case.

While investigating, he discovered that the shell company was registered in a tax haven, and the main contact was a person known as **Martín Salgado**, a specialist in money laundering. Lucas knew that he had to find Martín to get answers about the final destination of the money and his relationship with Andrea's murder.

At the end of the day, Lucas came across a clue that led him to an address in the center of town. The address belonged to an accounting office that appeared to be related to the shell company. He decided he should investigate the place before it closed.

He arrived at the office and, after a brief conversation with staff, discovered that Martín Salgado was in a meeting at a nearby branch. He went to the branch and, after presenting his identification, managed to talk to Martín.

Martín, a man in his 40s with a professional and calculating attitude, received Lucas with a mixture of disdain and curiosity. "Hello, Eduardo. How can I help you?"

Lucas was direct. "I'm investigating a murder case and I've found a connection between your company and the suspicious transactions. I want to know more about the funds and transfers that were made."

Martin frowned and tried to remain composed. "My company is in charge of financial services and accounting. If there's a problem, I'm not aware."

Luke showed the documents and evidence he had gathered. "These records suggest that your company is involved in money laundering to cover up illegal activities. Can you explain how your company is related to these payments?"

Martin seemed to be struggling with his words. "What I can tell you is that I handle a lot of transactions and contracts. If there are irregularities, I was not aware. My job is to conduct financial transactions according to the instructions of the clients."

Luke observed that Martin was not being completely transparent. "If you're not directly involved, who could be behind these transactions? Is there anyone else in your company who might know more about this?"

Martín was evasive and did not provide more information. Lucas decided that he should continue investigating and look for more clues in the financial environment. He knew that each piece of the puzzle brought him closer to the truth.

With the information obtained from Martín and the documents reviewed, Lucas returned to his apartment, prepared to continue unraveling the web of deception that surrounded Andrea's case. The connection between the financial transactions and the murder was taking shape, and Lucas was determined to see the investigation through to the end.

Chapter 10: The Enigma of Contacts

Lucas Ferrer stood at the top of an office building in the center of town, the wind blowing hard as he took in the panoramic view. The information gathered so far had been valuable, but he still had many loose ends to join. It had established that the suspicious payments and shell companies were part of an elaborate money-laundering scheme. However, the connection between these financial movements and Andrea's murder remained unclear.

He decided it was time to pay a visit to someone who could provide him with a different perspective on the case. He went to the office of **Diana Montero**, an investigative journalist who had covered several corruption and money laundering cases in the past. Diana was known for her keen intuition and her ability to uncover hidden truths.

Arriving at Diana's office, Lucas was met with a modern and elegant reception. The receptionist led him to a waiting room with magazines and newspapers. After a few minutes, Diana appeared, a woman in her 40s with a sharp gaze and a determined attitude.

"Hello, Lucas. What brings you here?" asked Diana, inviting him to sit down.

Lucas wasted no time in explaining his situation. "I am investigating Andrea's murder, and I have found a money laundering network and shell companies. I need your help to connect the dots and better understand the structure behind it all."

Diana listened carefully and nodded. "I can help you with that. I've been investigating similar cases and I might have information that could complement what you've found. But first, I need to know more about how you came to this information."

Lucas showed him the documents and emails he had collected, including financial transactions and connections between the security firm and the Ramirez Group. Diana examined the documents carefully, her expression becoming more and more serious.

"These documents are very revealing. Cash payments and transfers to offshore accounts indicate a fairly elaborate operation. But to understand the full scheme, we need to find the key people involved and see how they fit into the plot."

Diana suggested that they investigate the contacts of Roberto Salazar, the man who had been in the money laundering network. "It could be helpful to get information about the connections and contacts that Roberto had. Often, corruption networks have several layers and key contacts that facilitate the operation."

Lucas agreed and decided that his next step would be to trace Roberto's contacts. Using the information from the documents and Diana's connections, they began searching for people related to Roberto and the shell company.

During the investigation, they found a key contact in the case: **Luis Hernández**, a former employee of the security company who had been fired under suspicious circumstances. Luis had worked closely with Roberto and could have crucial information about the covert operations.

Lucas and Diana decided to visit Luis at his residence, located in a modest neighborhood south of the city. Luis's house was in disrepair, and it seemed like he was trying to keep a low profile. Upon arrival, Lucas and Diana introduced themselves and explained the reason for their visit.

Luis, a man in his 50s with a discouraged attitude, received them with distrust. "I don't know what I can tell you. My job at the company ended badly, and I don't have much to offer them."

Lucas was understanding but persistent. "We need to understand what you know about Roberto Salazar's transactions and contacts. Your perspective could help us solve the case."

Luis sighed and nodded. "I worked at the security company for years and knew Roberto very well. I know that he had a network of contacts that handled covert operations. Payments and contracts were always in cash, and there was a lot of money flowing through offshore accounts."

"And what about Roberto's contacts? Can you tell us something about them?" asked Diana.

Luis thought for a moment. "One of Roberto's closest contacts was **Victor Morales**, a man involved in the management of funds and the organization of special events. It was also related to money laundering and suspicious transactions."

Lucas and Diana took note of this information and said goodbye to Luis, thanking him for his help. They knew that Víctor Morales could be a key player in the resolution of the case. They decided to track down Victor and get more details about his involvement in the corruption network.

At the end of the day, Lucas and Diana returned to their respective offices, intending to further investigate Victor Morales and his relationship to the money laundering scheme. The connection between shell companies, money, and Andrea's murder was beginning to take shape, but there were still many pieces to fit together.

Chapter 11: The Network of Víctor Morales

Lucas Ferrer and Diana Montero met in a quiet café to discuss their next move. The information obtained from Luis Hernández about **Víctor Morales** seemed to be a key piece in the investigation. Victor Morales, it seems, was deeply involved in money laundering and the organization of covert operations. Knowing more about him could unravel the connection between the money and Andrea's murder.

Diana, with her ability to investigate, had begun to search for information about Victor. "I have found that Víctor Morales is a well-known figure in the world of finance and exclusive events. He has a company that organizes high-profile events and appears to be involved in several legitimate and dubious businesses."

Lucas leaned forward, interested. "And how can we track him down and find out more about his role in the case?"

Diana was thoughtful. "Victor has several properties in and around the city. He often organizes events in exclusive locations. We could start by investigating its properties and recent events. Perhaps there is something that will give us clues about his relationship with the shell company and the suspicious transactions."

They decided their best option was to investigate Victor's properties and attend one of his events, hoping to get direct information or some clue about his connection to the case. Lucas and Diana split the tasks: Lucas would focus on tracking down the properties, while Diana would try to infiltrate one of the events organized by Victor.

Lucas began his investigation by visiting several of Victor's properties, which included a mansion on the outskirts of town and an office in the business center. Upon arriving at the mansion, he found an imposing building surrounded by high walls and security cameras. He couldn't get much information directly, but he took note of the address and decided it would be helpful to review it further.

He then headed to the office in the business center, which was located in a modern and luxurious building. The office had a flawless appearance and was filled with employees working on different projects. Lucas approached the reception area and requested information about Víctor Morales. The receptionist, though courteous, didn't provide much information, but Lucas managed to get the card from a key employee: **Carla Nunez**, Victor's personal assistant.

Meanwhile, Diana was attending one of the events organized by Víctor Morales. It was an exclusive gala in an elegant hotel in the city. Diana, with a sophisticated appearance, managed to blend in with the attendees and began to ask discreet questions about Victor. During the gala, she noticed that Victor seemed to be in constant contact with several people and that there were a lot of suspicious interactions.

Diana approached a group of people who seemed to be discussing financial and business issues. Among them, he recognized **Andrés Martínez**, a well-known financier with connections in the world of money laundering. Diana decided to strike up a conversation with Andrew, hoping to learn more about Victor and his activities.

"Hello, Andrés. It's nice to meet you," Diana said with a friendly smile. "I've heard a lot about you and tonight's event. How did you get involved in this circle?"

Andrés, surprised by the question, answered cautiously. "It's a pleasure to meet you too. This event is just one of many activities we participate in. Víctor Morales is a very influential man and has connections in different business areas. He's always on the move and handling multiple trades at the same time."

Diana tried to dig deeper. "Do you know anything about Victor's connections with international companies or offshore accounts? I have heard rumors about his involvement in suspicious transactions."

Andrew was evasive but not completely disinterested. "Víctor handles a large amount of money and has relationships with various contacts. If you're researching something, I'd recommend talking to them directly. The information you seek could be in their hands."

Diana thanked the information and continued to observe the event. He managed to notice that Victor was having a private conversation with a group of people at the end of the night. He crept over and overheard parts of the conversation, which included mentions of money transfers and secret deals. It appeared that Victor was organizing a sting operation involving funds and cash payments.

At the end of the event, Diana and Lucas met to share what they had discovered. Lucas told Diana about Carla Núñez's card and information about Victor's properties. Diana informed him about the conversation she had overheard and mentions of suspicious transactions.

"I think Carla Nunez could be our next key," Lucas said. "If we manage to talk to her, we could get more details about Victor's activities and his connection to the money laundering network."

Diana agreed and they decided that their next step would be to contact Carla Núñez and find out more about her relationship with Víctor. The web of corruption was getting closer and closer to being unraveled, and Lucas and Diana were determined to see the investigation through to the end.

Chapter 12: The Interview with Carla Núñez

Lucas Ferrer and Diana Montero met early in the morning at a nearby cafeteria to plan their next move. After the gala and the information obtained from Andrés Martínez, they knew that the next crucial step was to contact **Carla Núñez**, Víctor Morales' personal assistant. Carla's card provided a direct entry point into Victor's close circle.

Lucas had managed to get Carla's contact number through a private investigator he knew, and they decided to call her to request a meeting. The phone rang several times before Carla answered.

"Hello, am I talking to Carla Núñez?" asked Lucas, trying to sound professional.

"Yes, it's me. Who's talking?" Carla replied, in an attentive but suspicious voice.

"Hello, Carla. My name is Lucas Ferrer and I am investigating a corruption and money laundering case involving Victor Morales. I would like to talk to you to learn more about his work and the contacts he manages," Lucas explained.

Carla paused before answering. "I understand. I'm not sure what I can tell you, but we could arrange a meeting. How about tomorrow at 10 a.m. in my office?"

Lucas accepted the invitation and was pleased with the response. Diana and Lucas planned their strategy for the meeting, making sure they were prepared to ask incisive questions and get as much information as possible.

The next day, Lucas and Diana arrived at Carla Núñez's office, located in an elegant office building in the center of the city. The front desk was modern and efficient, and they were soon ushered into Carla's office. The assistant, a woman in her 30s with a professional attitude, greeted them and offered them coffee as they prepared for the conversation.

Carla was cordial but reserved. "Thank you for coming. How can I help them?"

Lucas began the conversation. "We are investigating a complex case involving Víctor Morales. We have found some irregularities in transactions and connections with shell companies. We want to better understand how their work works and who is involved in these operations."

Carla listened carefully, but her expression didn't show much. "Victor is a very busy person and handles a variety of issues. My job is to organize your schedule and make sure everything runs smoothly. I don't have direct access to the details of financial transactions."

Diana intervened. "Could you tell us if you've noticed any unusual activity or transactions that have seemed strange to you in the last few months? Sometimes small details can be important clues."

Carla frowned as she thought. "I don't remember anything specific, but Victor has been handling a lot of funds for international events and special contracts. Payments and transfers are a routine part of their job."

Lucas noticed that Carla was being evasive. "Do you know if Victor has had any recent meetings with people from shell companies or offshore entities?"

Carla looked uncomfortable. "I am not aware of all the meetings, but Victor usually deals with high-level matters in private. I don't have details about the specific participants."

The conversation progressed without revealing much concrete information. Lucas and Diana decided that although Carla didn't provide clear answers, it was evident that there was something else beneath the surface. They thanked Carla for her time and said goodbye.

Leaving the office, Lucas and Diana discussed the meeting. "Carla didn't tell us much, but she seems to be aware of something without wanting to tell us directly," Diana observed. "It could be that he doesn't have permission to talk about certain issues or that he just doesn't want to get involved."

Lucas nodded. "It seems that Victor is handling this network very carefully. We need to find another way to get information, perhaps through other contacts or by digging deeper into their properties and activities."

They decided that the next step would be to further investigate Victor Morales' properties and activities, as well as track down any hints of secret meetings or hidden transactions. They knew that Andrea's case was increasingly intertwined with the web of corruption, and they were determined to uncover the truth behind the money laundering and murder ring.

Chapter 13: The Shadow of Truth

Lucas Ferrer and Diana Montero were in Diana's office, reviewing the documents and notes collected so far. The meeting with Carla Núñez had been frustrating, but it had given them a new direction to continue investigating. Carla's evasiveness indicated that Víctor Morales could be more involved in the case than they had initially thought.

Diana, who had continued to investigate Victor's network, found additional information about a company related to him, **Eventis Group**, which specialized in organizing high-profile events. The company had several branches in different cities and a number of international contracts. The information seemed to indicate that Eventis Group was involved in financial movements that matched the suspicious transactions Lucas had discovered.

"We need to investigate more about Eventis Group," Diana said, pointing to the information on her screen. "Víctor Morales has a direct relationship with this company, and it seems that he handles large sums of money through it. It may be that suspicious transactions and shell companies are connected through Eventis Group."

Lucas agreed. "We are going to investigate the offices of Eventis Group and analyze their financial records. We also need to find out if there are any key contacts who can provide us with more details about Victor's operations."

They decided to visit one of the Eventis Group branches, located in an elegant building in the financial district. The office had a professional and sophisticated atmosphere, with staff working on event planning and handling different projects. Lucas and Diana introduced themselves at the front desk, explaining that they were conducting an investigation into the company and requesting access to financial records.

The receptionist, with a professional expression, informed them that they would need an appointment to access the financial information. Lucas and Diana dropped off their cards and offered to schedule a meeting with the branch manager. Even though the front desk was courteous, they knew that accessing sensitive information would require more than just a request.

They then decided to do a parallel investigation into the structure of Eventis Group. Diana discovered that the company had a number of subcontractors and third-party suppliers that could be involved in the operations. Among them, they identified **Ricardo Soto**, a financial consultant with experience in the organization of international events and who had connections with several offshore entities.

Lucas and Diana decided to look for Ricardo Soto to interview him. Their search led them to a stylish office in an exclusive business area. Ricardo, a man in his 50s with a sophisticated appearance, was in the middle of a meeting when Lucas and Diana arrived. The receptionist asked them to wait in a conference room while Ricardo finished his meeting.

When Richard finally left, Lucas and Diana introduced themselves and briefly explained the reason for their visit. Ricardo, though initially evasive, seemed intrigued by the subject.

"What brings you here?" asked Ricardo, as he settled into a chair in front of them.

Lucas stepped forward. "We are investigating money laundering and corruption involving Eventis Group and Victor Morales. We have found some irregularities in the transactions and wanted to talk to you about your role in the company and your connections with offshore entities."

Ricardo frowned. "My work is focused on advising on event planning and financial management. I have no direct control over transactions or offshore connections. However, I can tell you that handling large sums of money is common in our industry."

Diana intervened, trying to dig deeper. "Do you know if Eventis Group has had any recent transactions or agreements that may be related to suspicious activity or shell companies?"

Ricardo looked thoughtful. "I'm not sure exactly what you're looking for, but sometimes large sums of money are handled to cover unforeseen expenses or for special events. If you're looking for something specific, maybe you should talk directly to those in charge of finance."

Lucas and Diana thanked the information and said goodbye to Ricardo. Although they did not get direct answers, the conversation provided them with a clue about the financial management and structure of Eventis Group.

Back at Diana's office, they reviewed the Eventis Group records and financial reports they had obtained. They found details about several large transactions and payments to offshore companies that matched the suspicious movements they had previously identified.

"There seems to be a pattern in the transactions," Diana said. "The payments and transfers are aimed at companies and accounts that could be involved in money laundering. This confirms our suspicions that Eventis Group is at the center of the corruption network."

Lucas nodded. "We need to continue investigating the connections between Eventis Group and shell companies. We should also explore the relationships between offshore entities and Victor Morales' contacts."

With the information obtained so far, Lucas and Diana were getting closer and closer to unraveling the network of corruption. They knew that Andrea's case was intimately tied to the covert operations and were determined to move forward until they uncovered the full truth behind the transactions and hidden contacts.

Chapter 14: The Closed Door

Lucas Ferrer and Diana Montero faced a new challenge. The information obtained about Eventis Group and the suspicious transactions confirmed that they were close to uncovering a much wider money laundering network than they had imagined. The connection to shell companies and offshore entities was beginning to take shape, but they needed more evidence to directly link Victor Morales to the illegal operations.

They decided to continue to thoroughly investigate Eventis Group's financial records, and to do so, they planned to gain access to the company's internal files. However, access to these documents was not going to be easy; They would require finding a way to infiltrate the records without raising suspicion.

Lucas and Diana began by identifying key Eventis Group employees who might have access to the sensitive files. In their investigations, they discovered that **Claudia Fernandez**, the company's chief accountant, had a history of handling large transactions and a reputation for being meticulous with financial documents.

"Claudia might be our best chance to get direct information," Diana said. "If we can gain their trust or find a way to access their files, we could get concrete evidence about the suspicious transactions."

Lucas and Diana decided to approach Claudia under the pretext of conducting external research for a report on the events industry. They contacted Claudia and managed to arrange a meeting at the Eventis Group office.

On the day of the meeting, Lucas and Diana showed up at Claudia's office, located in a less visible part of the building. Claudia's office was small but tidy, filled with meticulously organized files and documents. Claudia, a woman in her 40s with a serious appearance, received them with a professional attitude.

"Thank you for coming. How can I help you today?" asked Claudia, as she invited them to sit down.

Lucas began to speak. "We're doing a report on financial management in the events industry and we wanted to talk to someone with experience in the field. We have heard that Eventis Group is one of the leading companies in the industry and wanted to get some perspectives on handling large transactions."

Claudia nodded. "I understand. I will be happy to provide general information on how we handle finances and transactions at Eventis Group. Is there anything specific you'd like to ask about?"

Diana, observing Claudia's surroundings, decided to ask more general questions about accounting procedures and handling international payments. Claudia explained how the company handled large sums of money for international events and how payments were arranged through a number of accounts and subcontractors.

Lucas and Diana asked detailed questions, but realized that Claudia was very careful about the information she shared. It seemed like she was hidden behind a façade of transparency, but there was something about her attitude that suggested she knew more than she was willing to reveal.

At the end of the meeting, Claudia offered them some general statistics and sample documents, but did not allow them access to the internal records they were looking for. Lucas and Diana thanked the information and said goodbye, although they knew that they had not yet reached the bottom of the matter.

"Claudia didn't give us direct access to the files, but I think she's hiding something," Diana said as they left the office. "His attitude suggests that he might be aware of suspicious transactions or even connections to shell companies."

Lucas nodded. "We need to find another way to gain access to financial files. Perhaps we should consider investigating other employees or even trying to infiltrate the office in some way."

They decided that their next step would be to continue investigating Eventis Group employees and look for ways to access financial documents without raising suspicion. They also considered using social engineering techniques to obtain additional information or collaborating with an insider within the company.

Meanwhile, Diana followed up on Claudia's contacts and connections, looking for any indications that she might have leaked information to outsiders or been involved in the illegal activities. The investigation was becoming increasingly complex, but Lucas and Diana were determined to uncover the truth behind the undercover operations and Andrea's case.

Chapter 15: The Shadow of the Informant

Lucas Ferrer and Diana Montero were determined to move forward with the investigation of Eventis Group and the money laundering network. The meeting with Claudia Fernandez had been a dead end, but they were determined to find a way to access crucial financial documents. The option of using an inside informant was becoming increasingly attractive, but they needed to find someone willing to collaborate.

While Lucas reviewed the information of Eventis Group employees, Diana set about looking for possible connections between employees and suspicious activity. During his research, he discovered that **Raul Ortega**, a young finance analyst at the firm, had been working on reviewing the international accounts and had access to many of the documents they were looking for.

Diana decided to make a profile of Raúl to find out more about him. He learned that Raul was a relatively new employee and that, despite his role at the company, he had some connections in the financial world that could be useful. Diana decided it was time to approach Raul to see if he could get first-hand information.

To do so, Diana decided to use a social engineering strategy. She assumed the identity of a freelance researcher interested in the financial sector and contacted Raúl to request an informal meeting. He contacted him through a professional network and explained that he was conducting a study on the impact of international finance on the events sector.

Raúl accepted the invitation for a meeting at a nearby cafeteria, where Diana arrived on time and with a friendly attitude. Raul, a man in his 30s with a relaxed appearance, was willing to talk.

"Hello, Raúl. Thank you for taking the time to meet with me," Diana said, as they sat at a table by the window. "I'm researching how event companies handle international finance, and I'm very interested in your prospects."

Raul seemed interested in the conversation and began talking about his experience at Eventis Group. "It's challenging work, especially with all the international transactions and contracts. There are a lot of details to take into account, and sometimes things can be quite complicated."

Diana tried to deepen the conversation. "How do they handle large transactions and payments to international suppliers? Are there any special processes to ensure that everything is in order?"

Raul was more open as he talked about the general procedures. "We make sure to follow a rigorous process for each transaction. There are regular internal controls and audits. However, sometimes things can be more complicated than they seem at first glance."

Diana decided to take advantage of the conversation to probe if Raúl had noticed anything unusual or if he had had access to documents that could be related to suspicious activities. "Have you ever seen anything that seemed strange to you in the documents or transactions you handle? Sometimes, small details can be important."

Raul paused, showing an expression of doubt. "I'm not sure what you mean. Most transactions follow established procedures. However, sometimes payments to suppliers are handled through international accounts that can seem a bit opaque."

Diana noticed Raul's hesitation and decided to change his approach. "Thank you for sharing that. I was wondering if you knew anyone who might have more information about how those international payments are handled. Sometimes, talking to someone with more experience can be helpful."

Raul looked thoughtful and finally said, "You could talk to Claudia Fernandez. She handles a lot of the accounting and could have a clearer view of the details."

The conversation ended and Diana said goodbye to Raúl, thanking him for his time. As she left the cafeteria, Diana reflected on the conversation. Raul had been helpful in providing the clue about Claudia, but it also seemed like there was something else he wasn't willing to share.

Back at the office, Lucas and Diana discussed the meeting with Raul. "Raul seems to be aware of some irregularities, but he was unwilling to provide further details," Diana said. "His advice about talking to Claudia could be a way to divert our attention or just a valid suggestion."

Lucas agreed. "We need to continue investigating Raul and see if there is any way to get more information from him. Perhaps we can find a way to access the documents he is handling or find out if there is something else behind his evasive attitude."

They decided that the next step would be to keep a close eye on Raul and explore other ways to gain access to financial documents. The web of corruption was increasingly intertwined, and Lucas and Diana were determined to unravel the truth behind the covert operations and Andrea's case.

Chapter 16: The Hidden Connection

Lucas Ferrer and Diana Montero were at a critical point in their investigation. The information obtained about Eventis Group and key employees had revealed a more intricate money laundering network than they expected. Claudia Fernández's evasiveness and the clues provided by Raúl Ortega led them to the need to delve deeper into the company's financial structure.

In order to obtain more information, Lucas and Diana decided to focus on the documents that Raúl had mentioned. Hoping that the Eventis Group documents could provide additional leads, they decided to further investigate the international connections and suppliers mentioned in the financial records.

Diana was tasked with investigating the offshore accounts related to the suspicious transactions. He used a variety of tools and contacts to track the flow of money and connections between accounts. In the process, he discovered a pattern of recurring payments to a consulting firm called **Global Consult**, which appeared to be involved in coordinating international events and had multiple connections to offshore entities.

Lucas, for his part, continued to investigate Raúl Ortega and Claudia Fernández, looking for any indication that they could be involved in illegal activities. While reviewing social media and activity logs, Lucas discovered a series of messages and posts from Raul that showed a close relationship with an important figure in the financial field, **Sergio Velázquez**, a well-known investment consultant and financial advisor.

Sergio Velazquez had been mentioned in several reports as an expert on money laundering and tax evasion, and had a reputation for working with high-profile clients. Lucas decided that an interview with Velázquez could provide valuable information about the corruption network.

Lucas and Diana contacted Sergio Velázquez and arranged a meeting at his office, a luxurious suite in the city's financial center. Velázquez's office was opulent, with panoramic views and elegant décor. When Lucas and Diana arrived, they were greeted by Velázquez himself, a man in his 50s with an imposing presence.

"Welcome. How can I help you?" asked Velázquez with a calculating smile.

Lucas took the initiative. "We are investigating a money laundering network involving Eventis Group and Victor Morales. We have found connections between your company and offshore accounts. We would like to understand more about how these transactions work and if there is anything that may be related to our investigations."

Velázquez leaned in his chair, watching Lucas and Diana with interest. "Money laundering and tax evasion are complex issues. Many times, consulting firms are used to structure transactions and move funds in a way that makes them appear legitimate. Offshore connections are a common part of this process."

Diana intervened. "Do you know anyone at Eventis Group or Global Consult who might be involved in these activities? We have found recurring payments to Global Consult and would like to know more about their role in these transactions."

Velázquez maintained a professional attitude. "Global Consult is a company that handles many international operations, and they may be involved in money laundering-related activities. However, I don't have specific information about their individual transactions."

Lucas, taking advantage of the opportunity, asked about his relationship with Raúl Ortega. "We have found that Raul Ortega, an analyst at Eventis Group, has connections with several offshore entities. Do you know if he has worked with your company or if he has any relationship with your contacts?"

Velázquez showed a growing interest. "Raúl is a promising young man. I have not worked directly with him, but he is known in the financial field. He could be involved in an operation that is related to money laundering."

The conversation continued without providing specific details, but Lucas and Diana felt they were on the right track. Velázquez seemed knowledgeable on the subject, but he was unwilling to offer concrete information without some kind of incentive.

After the meeting, Lucas and Diana returned to their office to analyze the information obtained. The connection between Global Consult, Raul Ortega, and offshore entities was beginning to take shape, but key pieces were still missing to complete the puzzle.

"Velázquez knows more than he let on," Diana said. "His relationship with Raul and knowledge of Global Consult indicates that there is a wider network involved."

Lucas nodded. "We need to continue researching Global Consult and explore more about Raul and Velazquez's connections. Perhaps we should also consider using surveillance techniques to obtain additional information."

They decided that the next step would be to conduct a more in-depth investigation into Global Consult and its operations, as well as trace the financial connections between the companies involved. The web of corruption was increasingly intertwined, and Lucas and Diana were determined to unravel the truth behind the hidden transactions and contacts.

Chapter 17: The Secrets of Global Consult

Lucas Ferrer and Diana Montero were immersed in a whirlwind of financial connections and hidden secrets. The recent investigation into Global Consult had revealed that this company could be the center of money laundering operations. With the intention of discovering more, they decided to delve into the world of Global Consult and explore its activities in depth.

The first step was to gain access to Global Consult's public records and financial reports. Diana used her contacts in the financial world to gain access to internal records that were not readily available to the public. It found that Global Consult had been involved in a series of complex international transactions involving multiple offshore entities and shell companies.

As Lucas and Diana analyzed the documents, they discovered that Global Consult had been hired to handle large sums of money through a network of shell companies. The records indicated frequent payments to accounts in tax havens, with little transparency in the origin and destination of the money.

The information obtained also included records of emails and internal communications from Global Consult, which showed conversations between employees of the company and key figures in the financial world. Among the documents, they found an email exchange between **Daniela Rivas**, a senior executive at Global Consult, and **Sergio Velázquez**, the financial consultant they had previously interviewed.

The emails contained details about specific financial operations and strategies for moving large sums of money without raising suspicion. The communications also mentioned **Antonio Ruiz**, a private banker who had been key in handling international transactions.

Lucas and Diana decided that their next step was to investigate Daniela Rivas and Antonio Ruiz to better understand their role in the laundering network. They learned that Daniela was known for her skill in structuring complex transactions and had a reputation for handling sensitive cases with discretion.

Diana, using her identity as a freelance researcher, contacted Daniela to request an interview about the financial practices at Global Consult. Daniela agreed to the meeting and arranged a date at a posh coffee shop near her office.

On the day of the meeting, Diana arrived at the cafeteria and waited for Daniela. When Daniela appeared, she was a woman in her 40s, elegant and with a confident attitude. They sat down at a secluded table and began the conversation.

"Hello, Daniela. Thank you for meeting with me. I'm researching how consulting firms handle international finance and would like to hear your perspective on best practices in the industry," said Diana.

Daniela smiled and was willing to talk. "It's an interesting topic. At Global Consult, we handle a variety of complex transactions, and it's important to ensure that everything is in order and compliant with regulations."

Diana tried to deepen the conversation, focusing on the specific procedures for handling international transactions and the use of offshore accounts. "How do they handle transactions through accounts in tax havens? Are there any special processes to make sure everything is in accordance with the laws?"

Daniela was cautious but responded. "We make sure to follow a rigorous process and work with banks and entities that comply with international regulations. Transparency and compliance are crucial for us."

Diana also tried to obtain information about Global Consult's relationship with Sergio Velázquez and Antonio Ruiz. "Can you tell me about your relationship with Sergio Velázquez and Antonio Ruiz? How do they influence Global Consult's operations?"

Daniela was evasive. "Sergio and Antonio are respected professionals in the field. We collaborate with them in various capacities, but I don't have specific details about their individual implications."

After the meeting, Diana and Lucas discussed the information obtained. The conversation with Daniela had been helpful in confirming that Global Consult was handling complex transactions, but had not provided specific details about the illegal activities.

"Daniela was cautious and didn't reveal much about internal operations," Diana said. "But his knowledge and connections to Sergio Velazquez and Antonio Ruiz are indicative that the stakes are higher."

Lucas agreed. "We need to continue investigating Antonio Ruiz and look for ways to obtain additional information about the transactions handled by Global Consult. We might also consider conducting surveillance to collect direct evidence."

They decided that their next step would be to investigate Antonio Ruiz and explore his relationship with Global Consult and laundering operations. The web of corruption was increasingly tangled, and Lucas and Diana were determined to unravel the truth and uncover those responsible behind the illegal activities.

Chapter 18: The Shadow of Antonio Ruiz

In order to advance their investigation into Global Consult and the money laundering network, Lucas Ferrer and Diana Montero decided to focus on Antonio Ruiz. They knew that Ruiz, a private banker with connections in the financial field, might have crucial information about the transactions and offshore accounts involved in the case.

Diana and Lucas began by researching Antonio Ruiz's career. They discovered that he was known in the banking sector for his skill in managing accounts in tax havens and his experience in handling large sums of money. He had a reputation for being very private and kept a low profile in the media, making it difficult to obtain direct information about his activities.

They decided to use a surveillance strategy to gather more details about their activities and connections. Diana began to follow Antonio Ruiz discreetly, observing his movements and his interactions with other professionals in the financial field. Meanwhile, Lucas took it upon himself to look for more information about his relationships and his network of contacts.

The surveillance revealed that Antonio Ruiz frequented an exclusive country house on the outskirts of the city, where he met with other professionals in the financial sector. Diana also discovered that Ruiz regularly attended social events and conferences where she often held private meetings with clients and colleagues.

One day, as Diana was looking at Ruiz's country house, she noticed a luxury vehicle arriving frequently. The vehicle was registered in the name of **Elena Martinez**, a renowned lawyer with a history of working on tax evasion and money laundering cases. Diana decided to investigate more about Elena Martínez to see if she was linked to Antonio Ruiz's activities.

Lucas, for his part, continued to investigate Ruiz's network of contacts and discovered that Elena Martínez had a close relationship with several businessmen and financial consultants. It also found that Elena had been involved in defending several high-profile cases involving money laundering, suggesting that she may have a major role in the corruption network.

Diana and Lucas decided that their next step should be to approach Elena Martínez to obtain more information about her links with Antonio Ruiz and the laundering network. Using her identity as a researcher, Diana contacted Elena and requested a meeting to discuss the impact of tax evasion on the financial sector.

Elena accepted the meeting and they met at an elegant restaurant, known for being a discreet meeting place for professionals in the financial sector. Elena, a woman in her 50s with an imposing presence, greeted them with a professional attitude.

"Thank you for meeting with me, Elena. I am investigating the impact of tax evasion and money laundering on the financial sector," Diana began. "I'm interested to hear your perspective on how these cases are handled and how they affect businesses and individuals."

Elena showed interest in the conversation and began to talk about her experience in the field. "Tax evasion and money laundering are serious problems that affect the integrity of the financial system. We work to make sure our clients comply with regulations and avoid legal issues."

Diana tried to deepen the conversation. "I've noticed that you work with a number of clients on tax evasion cases. Is there a particular aspect that you think is important to understanding how these cases are handled?"

Elena spoke in a general way about legal procedures and strategies for handling complex cases. "Every case is different, and it's important to follow the regulations and procedures in place to ensure everything is in order."

Diana also tried to obtain information about her relationship with Antonio Ruiz and his role in financial transactions. "Do you have any relationship with Antonio Ruiz or Global Consult? I have found that they have links to several cases of tax evasion."

Elena was evasive and said: "Antonio Ruiz is a respected professional in the financial field. We collaborated in some cases, but I don't have specific details about their activities."

After the meeting, Diana and Lucas discussed the information obtained. The conversation with Elena Martínez had been useful in confirming that she was involved in the financial sphere, but did not provide concrete details about the illegal activities.

"Elena was evasive and didn't reveal much about her connections to Antonio Ruiz," Diana said. "But his relationship with Ruiz and his work on tax evasion cases indicates that there is a wider network behind the illegal activities."

Lucas agreed. "We need to continue investigating Elena and Antonio Ruiz, and consider conducting closer surveillance to obtain direct evidence of their activities. The web of corruption is becoming more complex, and we are getting closer to uncovering the truth."

They decided that their next step would be to continue the surveillance of Antonio Ruiz and Elena Martinez, and further explore their connections to Global Consult and financial transactions. The web of corruption was increasingly intertwined, and Lucas and Diana were determined to unravel the truth and expose those responsible.

Chapter 19: Revelations in the Country House

Lucas Ferrer and Diana Montero were determined to unravel the money laundering network that stretched through Antonio Ruiz and Elena Martinez. After several weeks of surveillance, they discovered that Ruiz had private meetings at his country house, where he met with important contacts in the financial field. The information obtained indicated that these meetings could be key to understanding the entire operation.

Diana had been following Ruiz and observed that on one occasion, a group of people arrived at the country house in luxury vehicles. Among them was **Francisco Delgado**, a well-known businessman in the pharmaceutical industry, whose company was under investigation for suspicions of corruption and money laundering. Delgado's presence in the country house aroused Diana's curiosity.

In order to obtain more information, Diana decided to infiltrate the country house during one of the meetings. She used a bold approach, presenting herself as a reporter interested in financial issues. He prepared to attend one of Ruiz's meetings under the guise of covering an exclusive event on investing and finance.

Diana dressed in smart clothes and carried a small tape recorder hidden in her bag to record any relevant conversations. With Ruiz's permission, he managed to enter the area where the meeting was to take place. The lodge was lavishly decorated, with a spacious conference room and a sophisticated atmosphere that reflected the status of the attendees.

As Diana mingled with the guests and watched the meeting from a discreet corner, she listened to snippets of conversation that talked about financial transactions, money laundering and structuring funds through offshore accounts. Participants discussed strategies for moving large sums of money without raising suspicion, and the conversation revolved around how to hide the true beneficiaries of transactions.

One of the main topics of the discussion was the creation of shell companies and the manipulation of financial records to give the appearance of legitimacy to transactions. Francisco Delgado and Antonio Ruiz were especially active in the conversation, suggesting methods to avoid detection and intervention by authorities.

Diana accurately recorded the important details of the conversation and, at the end of the meeting, managed to leave the country house without raising suspicion. He knew that the information he had obtained could be crucial in unraveling the web of corruption and exposing illegal activities.

When Diana returned to Lucas' office, she shared the recording and details of the meeting. Both were surprised by the amount of information they had obtained and the clarity with which money laundering techniques had been discussed.

"This is bigger than we imagined," Lucas said, as he reviewed the recording. "The way they talk about creating shell companies and manipulating financial records indicates a highly sophisticated operation."

Diana nodded. "Francisco Delgado and Antonio Ruiz seem to be key players in this network. We also need to find out how Elena Martinez is involved in all of this and if there are more people in the operation."

Lucas and Diana decided that the next step would be to analyze the recording for additional clues and prepare a detailed report on the activities of the laundering ring. They also planned a strategic approach to approach Elena Martinez and Francisco Delgado to learn more about their roles in the operation.

The web of corruption was becoming more intricate, and Lucas and Diana were determined to follow the trail until they uncovered the whole truth. With the information obtained at the country house, they were one step closer to unmasking those responsible and bringing them to justice.

Chapter 20: The Confrontation

The revelation obtained in Antonio Ruiz's country house had given a significant turn to the investigation of Lucas Ferrer and Diana Montero. With evidence of the sophisticated money laundering network and the connections between Antonio Ruiz, Francisco Delgado, and Elena Martinez, they were ready to take a crucial step: directly confronting Elena and Francisco to obtain more information and evidence.

Lucas and Diana decided that the best strategy was a calculated confrontation. They agreed that Lucas would approach Francisco Delgado in his office, while Diana would be in charge of confronting Elena Martínez in her office. The idea was to get direct answers and force both to reveal more about the illicit operation.

Diana arrived at Elena Martinez's office in a luxury skyscraper in the city's financial center. He had prepared himself carefully, keeping in mind the evidence and the recording obtained at the country house. Elena's office was elegant, with large windows that offered a panoramic view of the city. Diana waited in the reception room until Elena received her in her office.

"Hello, Elena. Thank you for finding time for this meeting," Diana said with a professional smile as they sat down in Elena's office.

Elena looked serene, but her eyes showed a hint of tension. "Hello, Diana. What would you like to talk about today?"

Diana, with a firm but diplomatic attitude, began. "I am investigating cases of tax evasion and money laundering. The information I have obtained suggests that you could be involved in a money laundering network that includes Antonio Ruiz and Global Consult."

Elena frowned, trying to keep her composure. "Where did you get that information?"

Diana took out a copy of the recording and put it on the table. "I have evidence of conversations between Antonio Ruiz, Francisco Delgado and other members of this network. The information you have about tax evasion and money laundering seems to be connected to these cases."

Elena examined the recording, and her face paled slightly. "Those conversations don't necessarily imply that she's involved in illicit activities. They may simply be discussing legal strategies."

Diana was not fooled. "The strategies discussed in the recording were clearly designed to evade detection by authorities and move money in a hidden manner. We need to know more about your role in all this and how you are linked to Antonio Ruiz and Francisco Delgado."

Elena leaned forward and spoke in a low voice. "I have nothing to hide. My job is to help my clients comply with regulations, and any information you may have heard should be misinterpreted."

Meanwhile, Lucas Ferrer was on his way to Francisco Delgado's office. Delgado's office was equally luxurious, with opulent décor and a large conference table. When Lucas arrived, he met Delgado in his office, who seemed relaxed and confident.

"Francisco, thank you for your time," Lucas began. "We are investigating a network of money laundering and tax evasion. The information we have obtained shows your involvement in this network, and we need to understand more about your role."

Delgado frowned, trying to maintain a cordial attitude. "What kind of involvement are you mentioning?"

Lucas put on the table a copy of the financial records and suspicious transactions that had linked Delgado to the illegal activities. "These documents show payments and transactions that are directly connected to money laundering. We want to know how you are involved and what your relationship is with Antonio Ruiz and Elena Martínez."

Francisco looked at the documents and his expression became serious. "Those documents could be part of legal operations. I can't comment on every detail without full context."

Lucas did not give in. "The evidence suggests that you are involved in a larger network of corruption. We need clear answers about how these transactions are carried out and who else is involved."

As the talks unfolded, Diana and Lucas continued to press Elena Martinez and Francisco Delgado for more information. Both showed resistance, but the evidence presented and pressure from the researchers made them increasingly uncomfortable.

At the end of the meetings, both Elena and Francisco were evasive, but the tension in the air and their hesitant answers indicated that they were hiding something. Diana and Lucas realized they were close to uncovering the full truth, but they still needed definitive proof to dismantle the money laundering network.

They decided that the next step would be to review the information obtained again and prepare a strategy to obtain additional evidence that could confirm the connections and involvement of Elena Martínez and Francisco Delgado. The web of corruption was about to be exposed, and Lucas and Diana were determined to follow the trail to the end.

Chapter 21: The Fissures in the Net

The day after the confrontations with Elena Martínez and Francisco Delgado, Lucas Ferrer and Diana Montero were in their office reviewing the information they had collected. The meetings had made it clear that Elena and Francisco were avoiding answering direct questions, and this increased Lucas and Diana's determination to obtain irrefutable evidence linking both to the money laundering network.

Lucas and Diana decided that the best way forward was to carry out a thorough analysis of the financial documents obtained and look for any clues that would confirm the connection between Elena, Francisco and Antonio Ruiz. They began by going through the recording and financial records again, paying special attention to any details that might have gone unnoticed.

Diana, while reviewing the recording, noticed a number of references to a company called **"Luminex Holdings"** in conversations between Antonio Ruiz and Francisco Delgado. This company, mentioned in the context of financial transactions, appeared to be a key player in the laundering network.

Lucas researched Luminex Holdings and found that it was an investment firm that operated in multiple countries and had a history of frequent changes in corporate structure. Luminex Holdings had been mentioned in previous reports about tax evasion and money laundering, but it had not been possible to directly link its operations to the individuals they were investigating.

They decided they needed to further explore Luminex Holdings to uncover its role in the money laundering network. Lucas was tasked with obtaining the information about the company's corporate structure and the people involved, while Diana focused on finding out more about the specific transactions associated with Luminex Holdings.

During his investigation, Lucas discovered that the company had ties to a bank in Switzerland known for its discretion in managing offshore accounts. It also found that Luminex Holdings had made substantial payments to shell companies that were related to the offshore accounts mentioned in the recording.

While Diana was reviewing transaction records, she found several payments that matched the dates and amounts mentioned in the recording obtained at Antonio Ruiz's country home. These payments were directed to accounts in tax havens and were associated with high-risk investments, indicating a possible attempt to hide the origin of the funds.

With this new information, Diana and Lucas realized that they were getting closer to unraveling the money laundering network. They decided that the next step should be to obtain direct evidence of the transactions and connection between Luminex Holdings, Antonio Ruiz, Elena Martínez and Francisco Delgado.

To obtain concrete evidence, they planned a strategy that included infiltrating an upcoming investor meeting hosted by Luminex Holdings. This meeting, which would be held at a luxury hotel, would be an opportunity to closely observe those involved and collect additional evidence.

Diana prepared to infiltrate the meeting as an investor interested in high-yield opportunities, while Lucas would handle surveillance from a position nearby. The investor meeting was an exclusive event, and Diana would have to use all her cunning to go unnoticed and obtain crucial information.

On the day of the meeting, Diana arrived at the hotel with a professional attitude and an appearance that matched that of the investors. She presented herself as a potential investor interested in the opportunities offered by Luminex Holdings. The meeting was held in an elegant conference room, where attendees discussed various investment opportunities and financial strategies.

Diana watched intently as the Luminex Holdings presenters discussed the characteristics of their investments and strategies for handling large sums of money. During the meeting, several financial transactions and strategies were mentioned that matched the details obtained in the recording and financial documents.

At one point, Diana noticed that Elena Martínez was present at the meeting, accompanied by Francisco Delgado. The presence of both confirmed that they were involved in the activities of Luminex Holdings, which strengthened the connection between them and the laundering network.

Diana took the opportunity to ask the presenters a few questions about investments and fund management strategies. Their questions were designed to elicit additional information and confirm the connections between Luminex Holdings and the individuals under investigation.

Meanwhile, Lucas, from his position of vigilance, watched Elena and Francisco interact with other attendees and make comments that confirmed their active participation in the meeting. Lucas took detailed notes and prepared a report on the activities observed during the meeting.

At the end of the day, Diana and Lucas met to discuss the findings. The information obtained at the investor meeting had provided additional evidence of the connection between Luminex Holdings, Elena Martinez, Francisco Delgado and the money laundering network. They knew they were getting closer to unraveling the truth and gathering enough evidence to expose corruption.

They decided that their next step would be to consolidate the information obtained and prepare a strategy for presenting the evidence to the authorities. The money laundering ring was about to be unmasked, and Lucas and Diana were determined to bring those responsible to justice.

Chapter 22: The Double Life of Elena Martinez

With the evidence gathered at the investors' meeting, Lucas Ferrer and Diana Montero decided to intensify their investigation into Elena Martinez. The information about his involvement in the money laundering network and his relationship with Luminex Holdings and other key individuals was disturbing. Lucas and Diana were determined to obtain definitive evidence confirming their role in the corruption scheme.

To better understand Elena's involvement, Diana focused on the personal life of the investigated. He discovered that Elena led a seemingly impeccable and respectable life, with a successful career in the financial sector and an impeccable public image. However, the evidence obtained suggested that his private life could hide a double life that connected to the illegal activities they were investigating.

Diana began to thoroughly investigate Elena's personal movements. He discovered that Elena had a secondary residence in an exclusive neighborhood on the outskirts of the city, which was not known to her colleagues or mentioned in her public profile. In addition, he learned that Elena frequently visited this place during the night, which aroused suspicion that she could be using the residence to carry out clandestine activities.

To learn more about Elena's secondary residence, Diana decided to pay a visit to the site. She presented herself as a prospective buyer interested in the property, using a meticulous approach to gather information without raising suspicion. During the visit, Diana observed that the house was equipped with advanced security systems and appeared to have a number of hidden rooms and offices.

Diana's investigation revealed that the secondary residence was equipped with a private office in which Elena likely managed aspects of the money laundering network. It found financial documents and transactions related to Luminex Holdings and other details that matched previously obtained evidence.

At the same time, Lucas continued with his investigation into the financial transactions and the structure of the laundering network. He discovered that

Elena Martínez had been involved in the creation of bank accounts in tax havens and the manipulation of financial records to hide the true beneficiaries of the transactions.

To corroborate the information, Lucas decided to conduct an inspection at the offices of Luminex Holdings, looking for more documents and records that would confirm the connection between Elena and illegal activities. In the offices, he found more evidence linking Elena to the suspicious transactions and money laundering methods.

Diana and Lucas met to discuss the findings and plan their next move. The evidence about Elena Martinez's double life was compelling and showed that she was deeply involved in the money laundering network. However, they knew they needed additional evidence and a solid strategy to confront Elena and present the evidence to authorities.

They decided that the next step would be to confront Elena with the new evidence obtained and pressure her to reveal more details about her role in the laundering network. They also planned to prepare a full report on the illegal activities and evidence they had gathered, to present to the authorities and ensure that the corruption network was dismantled.

The challenge they faced was great, but Lucas and Diana were determined to expose the truth and bring those responsible to justice. The money laundering network was about to be dismantled, and the confrontation with Elena Martinez would be a crucial step in the process.

Chapter 23: The Final Confrontation

Lucas Ferrer and Diana Montero were at a critical point in their investigation. With evidence of Elena Martinez's involvement in the money laundering ring, it was time for a final confrontation. The intention was to pressure Elena to reveal the truth and completely dismantle the corruption network they had been investigating.

Lucas and Diana decided to summon Elena Martínez to a meeting in a neutral location, away from her usual surroundings. They chose a fancy café in the center of town, hoping that the casual atmosphere might make Elena feel more comfortable and less defensive. The place offered a quiet atmosphere, ideal for a crucial conversation.

Diana arrived at the café before Elena to make sure everything was ready. As I waited, I would go over the evidence they were going to present and the key points I needed to address during the conversation. The strategy was clear: confront Elena with the information they had obtained, show her that there was no way to deny their involvement, and force her to reveal the remaining details of the network.

Finally, Elena arrived at the café. Although he tried to maintain a relaxed attitude, his expression showed signs of tension. Diana greeted her with a smile and guided her to a private table in a corner of the premises, where Lucas was already waiting.

"Hello, Elena," Diana said as they sat down. "Thank you for coming. I would like to discuss some important points with you."

Elena nodded, trying to hide her nervousness. "Of course, Diana. What is it about?"

Lucas, with a firm but calm attitude, began the conversation. "Elena, we have been investigating a money laundering network that includes several people and entities. The evidence we have obtained clearly shows your involvement in this scheme."

Diana took out a folder with documents and transcripts of the recordings. The folder contained evidence about financial transactions, Elena's involvement in Luminex Holdings, and her double life. Diana placed the folder on the table and began to review the documents.

"These documents show your direct connection to illegal activities. We have found evidence that indicates that you have been managing accounts in tax havens and carrying out transactions to hide the origin of the funds," Diana said with determination.

Elena looked at the documents with growing concern. "This doesn't prove anything. They can be misinterpreted or even forged documents."

Lucas, without losing his calm, answered. "The evidence is clear and corroborated by multiple sources. In addition, the recording we obtained shows conversations that confirm your involvement in money laundering."

Diana added: "We know that the secondary residence we have talked about is also involved in the network. We found documentation and records that link your activities to the laundering operation. Clearly you have a crucial role to play in all of this."

Elena, visibly agitated, tried to stay in control. "I have nothing to say. The accusations are unfounded and there is not enough evidence to implicate me."

Lucas and Diana looked at each other briefly, aware that Elena was trying to divert attention. It was crucial to push her to get the information they needed.

"We understand that this is difficult to accept," Lucas said, "but we intend to present this evidence to the authorities. If you cooperate and disclose all the information about the network, you might have the opportunity to negotiate your situation."

Elena was silent for a moment, assessing the implications of the offer. The pressure and evidence were overwhelming, and he knew that his position was increasingly precarious.

Finally, Elena relented. "It's okay. If cooperating means I'll have a chance to negotiate, then I'm going to talk. But I need to know that there is a possibility to reduce the consequences."

Diana and Lucas nodded, knowing that Elena's cooperation could be key to completely dismantling the laundering network. The information he would provide was essential to connect all the dots and bring the others involved to justice.

"We will work out the details of your cooperation," Diana said. "We will ensure that your testimony is taken into account and that the circumstances of your participation are considered."

The conversation ended with Elena agreeing to cooperate. Lucas and Diana prepared to present all the evidence and testimonies to the authorities. The money laundering network was about to be fully exposed, and the next step would be to confront the other members of the operation and ensure that all those responsible were brought to justice.

Chapter 24: Elena's Revelations

Elena Martinez, now committed to cooperating with Lucas Ferrer and Diana Montero, was ready to unravel the money laundering network that had been operating in the shadows. The decision to cooperate was made in the hope of reducing the potential legal consequences, but it also meant that it had to reveal details that would put many of its associates at risk and expose the web of corruption.

Lucas and Diana arranged a meeting with Elena in a safe and discreet place, where they could discuss and document all the information she was willing to provide. They chose a secluded boutique hotel on the outskirts of the city, known for its privacy and security. The meeting would be held in a private conference room, without the presence of third parties.

Elena arrived at the hotel with a grave expression, but at the same time, with a sense of relief knowing that she was collaborating to unmask the network in which she was involved. Diana and Lucas greeted her and led her to the conference room, where they sat around a table to begin the conversation.

"Thank you for your willingness to cooperate," Lucas said as they sat down. "We are going to review all the information you have and clarify all the details necessary for our investigation."

Elena nodded and began to speak in a serious tone. "What I'm going to tell you is only one part of the network. The operation is much more extensive and complex than you can imagine. My main role has been to manage transactions and accounts in tax havens."

Diana opened her notebook and began to take notes while Elena spoke. "Tell us as much as you can about transactions and how they're structured. We want to understand the full scope of the operation."

Elena explained that the network was made up of several layers of fraudulent operations. First, offshore accounts were used to receive large sums of money that actually came from illegal business and bribes. These accounts were kept under fake names and shell companies to avoid detection.

"Shell companies," Elena continued, "are used to justify money transfers. They are created to look legitimate and are linked to fictitious investors. The true source of the funds is concealed through a series of complex transactions and transfers across multiple countries."

Elena provided a list of names and addresses associated with the shell companies and bank accounts, along with details about the people behind them. He also handed over a series of documents and records containing crucial information about the transactions.

"In addition," Elena added, "Luminex Holdings acts as the nerve center of the operation. It is the company that coordinates the flow of money and ensures that transactions are kept hidden. Antonio Ruiz and Francisco Delgado are key players in the management and supervision of operations."

Lucas reviewed the documents and records provided by Elena, confirming that the information was consistent with the evidence they had already gathered. He also noted that some names and addresses match previous reports on shell companies and offshore accounts.

"This is very valuable," Diana said as she reviewed the documents. "We now have a clearer view of how the network is structured and who is involved. We also need you to provide us with details about the meetings and key contacts in the operation."

Elena explained that the meetings were held in discreet and safe places, such as private clubs and protected residences. It also provided information on key contacts who maintained constant communication to coordinate operations and manage funds.

"Antonio Ruiz is the one who makes the important decisions and oversees the laundering network," Elena said. "Francisco Delgado is in charge of financial operations and ensuring that funds move through accounts efficiently. There are other individuals involved who act as intermediaries and facilitators."

With this information, Diana and Lucas began to map out the connections and structure of the money laundering network. Elena's cooperation had provided a significant breakthrough in the investigation, but they knew there was still work to be done to secure the conviction of all those involved.

They decided that the next step would be to present the evidence to the authorities and coordinate an operation to capture the main perpetrators. The money laundering ring was about to be dismantled, and Lucas and Diana were determined to carry out the operation as accurately as possible.

Elena's revelation had been crucial to the progress of the investigation. With detailed knowledge of the operation and key connections, Lucas and Diana were one step closer to fully unraveling the web of corruption and ensuring that all those responsible face justice.

Chapter 25: The Plan in Motion

Elena Martinez's collaboration had been a major breakthrough in the investigation, but now was the time to act with precision to dismantle the money laundering network. With the information he had provided, Lucas Ferrer and Diana Montero were ready to present the evidence to the authorities and coordinate an operation that would bring the main perpetrators to justice.

Lucas and Diana met with a team of law enforcement officers and prosecutors to plan the operation. It was crucial that every detail be carefully coordinated to ensure that suspects were not alerted and that the evidence necessary for a successful conviction was obtained.

The meeting was held in a conference room at the police headquarters, with the presence of a select group of investigators and prosecutors specializing in corruption and money laundering cases. Lucas and Diana exposed all the evidence gathered so far, including the information provided by Elena, financial documents, and recordings.

"With the information we have," Lucas began, "we can demonstrate the existence of an extensive money laundering network involving various individuals and entities. Elena Martinez has provided crucial details about Luminex Holdings' transactions and operations, as well as the network's structure."

Diana continued, "We also have records that show how large sums of money have been moved through offshore accounts and shell companies. We need to ensure that the operation is executed accurately so as not to alert those involved and ensure that the necessary evidence is obtained at the right time."

The group of investigators and prosecutors reviewed the information and discussed the plan of action. They decided that the operation would be carried out in several phases: the first phase would consist of the capture of the main perpetrators, including Antonio Ruiz and Francisco Delgado, and the second phase would consist of the collection of additional evidence in their residences and offices.

The operation was scheduled for the next day. Teams would split up to coordinate actions in different locations simultaneously, ensuring that there was no chance of escape for suspects. Lucas and Diana would be in charge of supervising the operation and coordinating with the teams on the ground.

Meanwhile, Elena Martínez was also under police protection. He was provided with additional security to ensure his well-being during the operation and to prevent any attempt at retaliation by those involved. Elena was nervous but determined to collaborate with the authorities.

The night before the operation, Lucas and Diana revised the plan once again, making sure every detail was in place. It was crucial that everything went according to plan to ensure the success of the operation and the capture of those responsible.

The next day, the operation began early in the morning. Police and prosecutor teams moved quickly and accurately, carrying out arrest and search warrants at previously identified locations.

At Antonio Ruiz's residence, agents found additional documents confirming his involvement in the money laundering network. The evidence found included transaction records, correspondence and details about shell companies. Antonio was arrested without incident and taken to the police station for questioning.

Simultaneously, at the Luminex Holdings office, agents conducted an exhaustive search. They found more evidence linking the company to the illegal operations, including suspicious financial transactions and documents related to offshore accounts. Francisco Delgado was also arrested and taken to the police station.

The operation was carried out effectively, and the main perpetrators were captured. Lucas and Diana met with prosecutors to discuss next steps in the legal process. The evidence gathered during the operation would be used to build a strong case against those involved and secure their conviction.

With the main perpetrators in custody and the evidence in hand, Lucas and Diana were ready to face the trial and present the case. The money laundering network had been dismantled, and justice was about to be served.

The operation had been a success, and the collaboration between Lucas, Diana and the authorities had led to the capture of those responsible for an extensive network of corruption. The next step was to face the judicial process and ensure that all those involved were brought to justice.

Chapter 26: The Confession of Antonio Ruiz

With the key perpetrators of the money laundering network in custody, the judicial process began to take shape. The arrests of Antonio Ruiz and Francisco Delgado had been successful, but in order to build a strong case, it was essential to obtain confessions and more information about the operation. The first great opportunity to advance in the case would come with the confession of Antonio Ruiz.

Antonio Ruiz was taken to an interrogation room at the police station, an austere space with white walls and a metal table in the center. Lucas Ferrer and Diana Montero prepared for the interrogation, with the intention of extracting as much information as possible. The tension was palpable, as the success of the case depended largely on Antonio's willingness to cooperate.

Lucas and Diana introduced themselves to Antonio, who was sitting at the table, visibly tired but defiant. Lucas began the conversation with a firm but professional tone.

"Antonio, we know you're aware of the serious allegations you're facing," Lucas said as he sat across from him. "We are here to listen to what you have to say and to come to a resolution. Your cooperation can influence the sentence you receive."

Antonio looked up, and although he seemed to be calculating his options, he didn't say anything at first. Diana intervened, softening the focus.

"Antonio, we have solid evidence that proves your involvement in money laundering and corruption," Diana said. "You don't have much room to continue denying it. If you cooperate and provide us with all the information you have, we might consider a reduction in potential penalties."

Antonio relaxed slightly in his chair, his expression changing to a mixture of resignation and calculation. "What you say is true. I was aware that the situation was complicated, but I thought I could handle it. However, it seems that things are getting out of control."

Lucas took advantage of the opening. "Tell us everything you know about the network. We need full details on how the operation works, who is involved and what mechanisms they use to launder the money."

Antonio nodded slowly, preparing to reveal crucial information. "Luminex Holdings is at the core of it all. Francisco Delgado and I oversaw the main operations. Francisco handles transactions and ensures that funds are moved through offshore accounts. I, for my part, was involved in strategic decision-making and coordinating activities with other partners."

Diana quickly took notes as Antonio continued. "Transactions are carried out through a network of shell companies that we have created to justify the flow of money. Most transactions are made through banks in countries with strict banking laws, making it difficult to trace funds."

"Who is behind the front companies?" asked Lucas. "Are there other key people we should know?"

Antonio hesitated for a moment, but then provided additional names. "There are several hidden investors and partners who keep a low profile. Some of them are middlemen who handle cash and are responsible for transferring funds between accounts. In addition, there is a network of contacts abroad that facilitates transactions."

"And what about Elena Martínez?" asked Diana. "What is your role in all this?"

"Elena is critical to the operation," Antonio replied. "She manages the accounts in tax havens and coordinates financial activities with us. Without their involvement, the network would not be able to function as efficiently."

Lucas and Diana exchanged glances, knowing that Antonio's information corroborated much of the evidence they had gathered. As the interrogation progressed, Antonio provided additional details about the methods used to conceal the transactions and the internal structure of the laundering network.

Finally, with the information provided by Antonio, Lucas and Diana felt that they were in a much stronger position to make the case against those involved. Antonio's confession not only strengthened the evidence against him, but also opened the door to obtain more evidence and move forward in the judicial process.

The next step would be to coordinate with prosecutors to prepare the case and make sure all the details were included in the indictment. Antonio's confession had been a crucial breakthrough, and Lucas and Diana were determined to bring the case to a successful conclusion.

Chapter 27: The Discovery at Francisco Delgado's Residence

With the crucial information gleaned from Antonio Ruiz's confession, Lucas Ferrer and Diana Montero prepared for the next step in their investigation: the search of Francisco Delgado's residence. They knew that additional evidence could be found in Delgado's home that would corroborate Antonio's statements and provide more details about the money laundering network.

Francisco Delgado's residence was located in an exclusive neighborhood, characterized by its luxury mansions and strict security. The house, with a modern and elegant design, stood with imposing white walls and large windows that offered panoramic views of the surroundings. Although the appearance was ostentatious, the real concern was to ensure that there were no elements that could alert Delgado about the operation.

Lucas and Diana arrived in the neighborhood with a team of police officers. The operation was carefully coordinated to ensure that the search was carried out effectively and without incident. The team split into groups to tackle different areas of the residence, including the offices, the security vault and the storage areas.

The operation began early in the morning, with the agents advancing silently towards the residence. Security at the entrance was quickly neutralized, and the team entered the mansion without any problems. Lucas and Diana headed toward Delgado's main office, where they hoped to find the most relevant evidence.

Francisco Delgado's office was decorated with high-end furniture and advanced technology. What Lucas and Diana were really interested in, however, were the documents and files that might be hidden in the office. Agents began meticulously searching the area, looking for any clues that might lead to the connection to money laundering.

Diana came across a series of filing cabinets on a hidden wall behind a bookshelf. He opened the files and began reviewing the contents while Lucas supervised the process. Among the documents, it found detailed records of financial transactions, correspondence with shell companies and contracts that confirmed Delgado's involvement in the fraudulent operations.

Meanwhile, another group of agents inspected the security vault in the basement of the residence. The vault was protected by a complex electronic lock that, after a brief effort, was opened by security experts. Inside the vault, they found safes filled with additional documents, as well as a large amount of cash in different currencies.

Lucas and Diana reviewed the documents found in the vault and confirmed that they contained crucial evidence about the flow of money and transactions made by Delgado. The files included bank reports, transfer records and details about accounts in tax havens.

"All of this reinforces what Antonio told us," Diana commented as she examined the documents. "Here we have additional evidence showing how the money has been moved and how the true source has been hidden."

Lucas nodded as he went through a specific folder containing information about the network's international connections. "These documents also seem to confirm the involvement of contacts abroad. We can use this information to trace the money internationally and find more evidence."

With the evidence gathered, the team continued the search of the residence, ensuring that no detail was overlooked. Eventually, the search operation at Francisco Delgado's home was successfully completed, and all evidence was collected and secured for further analysis.

The next step would be to present the evidence to prosecutors and prepare the case for trial. The information found at Delgado's residence further strengthened the accusation against him and provided a clearer view of the money laundering network.

Lucas and Diana were pleased with the progress of the investigation, knowing that every piece of evidence obtained was crucial to bringing those responsible to justice. With the case moving forward, the team was getting closer and closer to closing the chapter on one of the most complex money laundering operations they had ever faced.

Chapter 28: The Trial of the Responsible

With the evidence gleaned from the records and confessions, Lucas Ferrer and Diana Montero were ready to present the case in court. The trial of Antonio Ruiz and Francisco Delgado was the next big step in the judicial process, and all the previous work would be concentrated on securing a conviction that reflected the magnitude of their crimes.

The courtroom was bustling with activity as he prepared for trial. The courtroom was spacious and formal, with an atmosphere full of tension. Journalists and media outlets were present, ready to cover the case that had captured public attention due to the scale of the money laundering operation and the names involved.

Lucas and Diana prepared to present the evidence. They had worked with prosecutors to prepare a strong case, and now it was time to prove the defendants' guilt with hard evidence. The courtroom was divided into two sections: the defense area and the accuser's area. Antonio and Francisco's defense attorneys were ready to present their arguments, while Lucas and Diana were prepared to present the evidence.

The trial began with the prosecution's presentation of the case. Lucas Ferrer, as an expert witness, took the stand and began to detail the evidence they had collected. He described how the money laundering network had been dismantled and how Antonio Ruiz and Francisco Delgado were implicated in the fraudulent operations.

"The evidence we present clearly and forcefully demonstrates the defendants' involvement in a complex money laundering network," Lucas said, pointing to the documents and records presented as evidence. "We have followed the money trail through offshore accounts, shell companies and financial transactions."

Diana Montero took the floor next, providing additional details on the network's operations and structure. He explained how the laundering network had been organized and how the defendants had coordinated activities to avoid detection.

"The information obtained during the investigation confirms that the defendants were at the center of the laundering operation," Diana explained.

"Financial records and transactions have been verified and corroborated with documentary evidence and testimonies."

During the presentation of the case, defense attorneys attempted to discredit the evidence, arguing that the evidence was inconclusive and that the confessions obtained could have been induced. However, the prosecution presented testimony from additional witnesses, including Elena Martinez, who confirmed the defendants' statements and provided a more detailed view of the operation.

Elena Martinez testified from a shielded witness room because of her collaboration with the prosecution. She recounted how she had been involved in the laundering network and confirmed the central role of Antonio Ruiz and Francisco Delgado in the operations. Her testimony corroborated the evidence presented and helped strengthen the case against the defendants.

The trial ran for several weeks, with a series of testimonies, evidence and arguments presented by both sides. Each day brought new developments and moments of tension as the court listened to the details of the case.

Finally, the trial came to a conclusion with the closing arguments of the prosecution and the defense. Lucas and Diana made one final presentation to summarize the evidence and highlight the guilt of the accused. The prosecution asked the jury to consider the magnitude of the crime and the strong evidence presented during the trial.

The jury deliberated for several hours before returning with a verdict. The courtroom was silent as the judge read the decision. The guilty plea of Antonio Ruiz and Francisco Delgado was greeted with a mixture of relief and satisfaction from those present.

The trial concluded with a firm conviction for both defendants. Antonio Ruiz and Francisco Delgado were found guilty of money laundering, corruption and other related charges. The case had been a success for the prosecution, and justice had been done.

Lucas and Diana were satisfied with the result. They had faced significant challenges during the investigation and trial, but their determination and hard work had paid off. With those responsible convicted, the next step would be to ensure that the appropriate penalties were applied and to continue with the necessary legal actions to ensure that the money laundering network was completely dismantled.

Chapter 29: The Repercussions on the Business World

With the conviction of Antonio Ruiz and Francisco Delgado, the money laundering network had officially been dismantled, but the repercussions of this case extended beyond the walls of the court. The fall of these two key individuals deeply affected the structure of Luminex Holdings and the business connections that had kept the operation going.

News of the conviction spread quickly through the media. Coverage of the case revealed details about the money laundering operation, and the public exposure had a significant impact on the business world. Luminex Holdings shares fell sharply in the stock market, and investors began to lose confidence in the company.

Lucas Ferrer and Diana Montero met in their offices to discuss the implications of the case. They knew that while the conviction was a major achievement, there were many more issues that needed to be addressed to bring the investigation chapter to a close.

"Now that the leaders of the network have been convicted, it's crucial to see how this affects the company and its operations," Lucas said as he reviewed media reports and market updates. "Luminex Holdings is in crisis, and there are a lot of moving parts at play."

Diana nodded, looking at the news highlighting the company's stock drop and comments from financial analysts. "The ramifications of this could be wide-ranging. Investors are worried, and the company will face a number of legal and financial problems. It's important that we keep an eye on how things develop."

Meanwhile, Elena Martínez, who had collaborated with the authorities during the case, was in the process of receiving additional protection due to threats received from network associates. Elena had decided to speak to the press about her experience, seeking to make a public statement that could contribute to her safety and the transparency of the process.

At a press conference, Elena addressed the media with courage. "My testimony was instrumental in dismantling the money laundering network that operated secretly in the business world," he said. "I hope that my experience will serve to prevent future crimes and to demonstrate that justice can prevail, even in the most complex cases."

Elena's statement generated a great deal of media attention, and her bravery was applauded by many. However, it also attracted the attention of those who might still be angry about the public exposure of its illicit operations.

Lucas and Diana continued to monitor the development of the situation at Luminex Holdings. The company was facing additional investigations and a series of lawsuits from shareholders and other affected parties. The impact of the fall of key executives was felt at all levels of the organization.

Elena also began to collaborate with other investigators who were investigating the network of international contacts involved in money laundering. The information he had provided was valuable not only for the current case, but also for the investigation of other similar networks operating abroad.

As the situation unfolded, Lucas and Diana realized that the case had been more far-reaching than they had initially anticipated. They had dismantled a complex network and put an end to a significant money-laundering operation, but the repercussions continued to spread.

The fall of Luminex Holdings and the impact on the market were evidence that the actions of those responsible had had a profound effect on the business world. Lucas and Diana prepared to move forward with their upcoming investigations and to address the legal and financial consequences of the case.

Chapter 30: The Last Traps of the Net

Although the conviction of Antonio Ruiz and Francisco Delgado had been a great achievement, Lucas Ferrer and Diana Montero knew that there were still crucial details to be resolved. The money laundering network had been dismantled, but there were still components of the operation that could be active or have left clues that could lead to the arrest of more involved.

With the evidence and documents obtained during the investigation, the team decided to further examine the financial records and transactions that had not been fully covered during the trial. The files discovered at Francisco Delgado's residence revealed a more extensive network of shell companies and offshore accounts, some of which had been partially traced.

Diana immersed herself in analyzing the financial data, looking for additional patterns or connections. As he examined a series of suspicious transactions, he noticed a series of recurring payments that didn't seem to fit the profile of well-known shell companies. These payments were made through a series of intermediaries and were destined for several accounts in a small tax haven.

Lucas joined Diana in the analysis, and together they decided to track these transactions through further investigation. The details led to a small island in the Caribbean, known to be a haven for covert financial activities. Lucas and Diana contacted a team of local investigators to learn more about the accounts and intermediaries involved.

Meanwhile, Elena Martínez continued with her protection process, but she was also willing to collaborate in the investigation. His experience and knowledge of the money laundering network was valuable, and Lucas and Diana asked him to help identify any potential connections that had gone unnoticed.

On the Caribbean island, the local investigative team found that some of the accounts were linked to high-profile individuals and shell companies that had operated in the shadows. It was revealed that some of these individuals had been using false identities and had established multiple layers of protection to avoid being tracked.

Lucas and Diana arranged a meeting with the local team to discuss the findings and plan next steps. The information gathered indicated that there was an additional protective structure at play, designed to conceal the true magnitude of the operation.

"All of this suggests that there is an additional layer in the network that we haven't fully touched," Lucas said as he reviewed the reports. "We need to unravel these links to understand who else is involved and how they are operating."

The local team on the island collaborated to obtain search warrants and begin tracing connections. Lucas and Diana prepared to go to the island to coordinate the operation and gather additional evidence. The task was not easy, as the network had been carefully designed to evade detection.

On their journey to the island, Lucas and Diana faced several logistical challenges, including legal barriers and the need to secure cooperation from local authorities. However, they were determined to expose the truth and complete the work they had started.

As they progressed in the investigation, they began to uncover additional documents and records that pointed to an even more extensive network of contacts. There were indications that some of the financial operations were being handled by intermediaries operating from abroad, and connections to international criminal organizations were revealed.

With each new piece of evidence, the case became more complex. Lucas and Diana knew they were close to unraveling the full web, but they were also aware that time and resources were limited. They needed to act quickly to prevent those responsible from escaping or destroying evidence.

The investigation was at a critical stage, and the team was prepared to face any obstacles that came its way. The money laundering network had proven to be more resilient and complex than initially thought, but Lucas and Diana were committed to bringing the investigation to its final conclusion.

Chapter 31: The Network Dismantled

The operation on the Caribbean island began with great intensity. Lucas Ferrer and Diana Montero, along with the local investigative team, had managed to secure a series of search warrants that allowed them access to various properties and offices associated with the discovered shell accounts and companies. Time was crucial, and every minute counted in the race to dismantle the money laundering network.

The first target was a posh office in an exclusive financial district on the island. The modern and neat façade contrasted with the hidden world that was inside. Lucas and Diana, equipped with their knowledge and the cooperation of local investigators, made their way to the entrance of the building while the team forced their way in an orderly and professional manner.

The office was full of files and documents that seemed harmless on the surface. However, Lucas and Diana knew that behind every folder and every record could be hidden crucial clues. While reviewing the documents, they discovered a series of contracts and transactions that confirmed the participation of several individuals in the laundering network.

One of the most revealing documents was a contract signed by several offshore entities detailing the transfer of large sums of money to accounts in different countries. The contract included details on the creation of shell companies that acted as a front for laundering. Diana underlined the importance of this document, which demonstrated the magnitude of the scheme and the sophistication of the operations.

As the team continued with the office search, Lucas received an urgent call from the team at another location. They had found a vault hidden in a nearby property, which contained safes filled with cash and more relevant documents. The magnitude of the find was significant and showed that the laundering network had been much wider than had been estimated.

With evidence in hand, Lucas and Diana coordinated with prosecutors to ensure evidence was presented in court. The information obtained on the Caribbean island provided a detailed view of the laundering network and its global ramifications. International collaboration and joint effort had made it possible to effectively dismantle the network.

As the investigation progressed, Lucas and Diana also faced an unexpected challenge. An attempt at sabotage arose when they realized that someone had tried to destroy some of the evidence they had secured. The internal investigation revealed that one of the network's intermediaries had attempted to remove critical evidence to avoid legal prosecution. Fortunately, the team had taken precautions and was able to recover the evidence in time.

With the laundering ring dismantled and evidence collected, the next step was to prepare charges against all those involved and ensure that those responsible were brought to justice. The operation had been successful, but Lucas and Diana knew that the work was not over. The investigation had revealed a global network of financial crime, and it was vital that the task of continuing to track down and dismantle any vestiges of illicit operations was continued.

Lucas and Diana's work had not only exposed the truth behind the money laundering scheme, but had also set a precedent for future financial corruption investigations. The network had been one of the most complex they had faced, but their determination and skills had led to justice's triumph.

Chapter 32: New Threats

With the dismantling of the money laundering network on the Caribbean island, Lucas Ferrer and Diana Montero believed they had completed their primary mission. However, a series of unexpected events began to jeopardize the safety of the investigation and those involved.

The first sign of trouble came when Lucas received an anonymous letter in his office. The message, written in a threatening tone, warned that if he and his team continued to investigate, there would be serious consequences. Although the letter did not contain specific details, the threat was disturbing enough to cause Lucas and Diana to reconsider their security measures.

Diana, upon receiving the news, took the initiative to strengthen protection measures. It reached out to local authorities and security experts to increase surveillance in the offices and homes of team members. In addition, they ensured that Elena Martinez was also under proper protection due to her crucial role in the case.

Meanwhile, the media continued to cover the impact of the fall of Luminex Holdings and the repercussions of the money laundering network. The reports were full of details about the international connections and the individuals involved. This public coverage was putting additional pressure on researchers and increasing the risk of retaliation.

Lucas and Diana decided to do a thorough review of the documents and evidence collected during the investigation to ensure that no key information had been overlooked. As they went through the files, they discovered new clues that suggested there were still important pieces of the puzzle to fit together.

Among the documents reviewed, they found a series of emails containing veiled threats towards several members of the team and their families. These emails came from an address that appeared to be associated with an intermediary in the laundering network. The information suggested that the group was still operational and that there were attempts to intimidate those who had exposed its activities.

Lucas and Diana decided to address the threat proactively. They reached out to their contacts in the field of intelligence and international security for additional assistance. Secure communication channels were established and protection measures were improved in all areas involved.

As the investigation continued, Lucas began receiving cryptic messages that appeared to be related to the threats received. These messages included vague clues and references to a "hidden truth" that had not yet been revealed. Although Lucas tried to decipher the meaning of these messages, the mystery only added to the tension in the team.

Meanwhile, Diana and Elena worked together to analyze the documents and emails in search of clues that could lead to those responsible for the threats. Elena's collaboration proved to be valuable, as she had been in contact with several members of the network and had a deep understanding of their operations and strategies.

The team decided to organize an emergency meeting to discuss the threats and next steps. During the meeting, the possibility that there was a final layer of the laundering network not yet discovered was discussed, and strategies were proposed to address any imminent threats.

Tension was mounting as the team prepared to face possible new complications. They knew they were dealing with a well-organized and dangerous group, and that the threat of retaliation was real. The safety and integrity of the investigation were at stake, and Lucas and Diana were determined to protect the progress made.

With the pressure mounting, the team focused on solving the mystery of the threats and ensuring that the money laundering network was completely dismantled. They knew that the success of the case depended on their ability to handle the situation and stay one step ahead of those trying to sabotage their work.

Chapter 33: The Labyrinth of Truth

The growing pressure and threats began to take a toll on Lucas Ferrer and Diana Montero's team. With the security measures reinforced, they faced a new stage of the investigation, in which each clue seemed to lead to more questions than answers. The last layer of the money laundering network appeared to be a maze of deception and sophisticated maneuvers.

Lucas, determined to uncover the truth behind the threats, began investigating the origin of the cryptic messages. Each clue appeared to be connected to a specific piece of evidence in the case. The threatening emails contained vague references to a "hidden truth" that Lucas said could be linked to an even broader scheme of corruption and cover-up.

Diana and Elena collaborated in the analysis of the documents related to the threats. While reviewing the evidence, they discovered a number of transactions that did not seem to fit with the rest of the money laundering scheme. These transactions were associated with a technology company that apparently had no connection to the previously discovered illegal operations.

The company in question, TechNex Solutions, was a technology service provider with a global presence. Although its operations appeared legitimate, there were indications that it could have been used to facilitate money laundering through encrypted data transfer systems and specialized software.

Lucas and Diana decided to further investigate the connection between TechNex Solutions and the laundering network. Through contacts in the technology sector, they began to obtain information about the company and its practices. They discovered that TechNex Solutions had been used to create a complex funds transfer system that allowed the movement of large sums of money without raising suspicion.

The investigation led Lucas and Diana to a series of meetings with current and former TechNex Solutions employees. As they delved deeper into the subject, they discovered that the company had been infiltrated by members of the laundering network, who had manipulated their systems to facilitate the cover-up of illicit financial transactions.

During one of these meetings, a former TechNex Solutions employee, named Javier Rios, revealed crucial information. Javier had worked in the company's software development department and had witnessed how the encrypted transfer system had been implemented to hide transactions. However, he had been under pressure from members of the network not to reveal what he knew.

Javier was willing to cooperate with the investigation in exchange for protection and guarantees that he would not be implicated in the illegal activities. His testimony provided details about how the software had been manipulated and how transactions were masked under layers of complex encoding.

Lucas and Diana organized an undercover operation to collect direct evidence of TechNex Solutions' activities. The team used Javier's testimony to obtain a search warrant for the company's servers and systems. The operation revealed a wealth of information about illicit transactions and TechNex Solutions' role in the global money laundering scheme.

While reviewing the data obtained, Lucas discovered a hidden file containing a list of international contacts linked to the network. These contacts included names of influential figures in the financial and political world, suggesting that the money laundering scheme had much broader connections than had initially been assumed.

The revelation of this information increased the urgency of the investigation. Lucas and Diana knew they were close to uncovering the full truth, but they were also aware that they were dealing with a powerful and dangerous network that would stop at nothing to protect their interests.

With the evidence in hand, the team prepared a detailed report to present to international authorities. The information gathered not only confirmed TechNex Solutions' involvement in money laundering, but also indicated that the network had global ramifications that needed to be addressed.

Chapter 34: In the Eye of the Hurricane

With crucial evidence about TechNex Solutions' involvement in the money laundering scheme, Lucas Ferrer and Diana Montero were ready for the next step in their investigation. The information revealed had elevated the case to a level of international exposure, and the danger of reprisals had increased. The pressure to close the case successfully was immense.

Lucas and Diana met with international authorities and shared the information obtained. The scale of the money laundering network, coupled with the high-profile connections, required global collaboration to carry out the necessary actions. Prosecutors and security forces from several countries joined the effort to prepare a series of arrests and coordinated operations.

As operations were being organized, the team received alarming news of sabotage attempts. Some of the members of the investigation team began receiving direct threats, and incidents of unauthorized surveillance in offices were reported. The laundering network appeared to be reacting to developments in the investigation, indicating that they were being closely monitored.

Lucas and Diana decided to take extra steps to protect themselves. They hired private security to protect their homes and offices, and made sure that all team members were under constant surveillance. The situation was becoming increasingly tense, and the feeling of being at the center of a relentless storm was palpable.

Meanwhile, Elena Martínez was working on a detailed report on the international contacts involved in the scheme. His knowledge of the key players in the laundering network was critical to understanding how they operated and to identifying potential allies within the global financial system.

The information gathered by Elena revealed that some of the international contacts were involved in the manipulation of financial markets and the financing of criminal operations. These discoveries increased the urgency of arrest operations and the need to dismantle the laundering network quickly and effectively.

Lucas and Diana prepared to coordinate a series of simultaneous raids in several key locations around the world. The operation was designed to dismantle the network's infrastructure, arrest major players, and secure crucial evidence before it could be destroyed or hidden.

On the morning of the operation, the team was ready to carry out the raids. Each team member was assigned to a specific location, and arrest warrants were issued internationally. Coordination between security agencies and local authorities was impeccable, and the operation was executed with precision.

The raids revealed a number of surprises. At one of the locations, documents were discovered indicating that the network had even wider ramifications than previously thought, with connections to criminal organizations on other continents. In another, clues were found that pointed to a possible leader hidden behind the scheme.

As the arrests were carried out, Lucas and Diana faced an additional challenge: securing the cooperation of the detainees and obtaining information about the hidden leader. Some of those arrested were willing to cooperate in exchange for reduced sentences, while others maintained a defiant attitude.

Lucas and Diana focused on interrogating key detainees to unravel the identity of the hidden leader and obtain details about the remaining operations. Interrogation sessions revealed that the network had been using multiple layers of covert operations to avoid detection.

The tension was palpable as the case neared its conclusion. The money-laundering network had largely been dismantled, but the search for the hidden leader and the complete dismantling of the network remained priorities. Lucas and Diana were determined to see the case through to the end and ensure that those responsible faced justice.

Chapter 35: The Final Revelation

With the arrest operation underway and the money laundering network practically dismantled, Lucas Ferrer and Diana Montero were at a crucial moment in the investigation. However, the search for the hidden leader and a full understanding of the network's reach remained essential to closing the case for good.

The interrogations of detainees had begun to provide valuable bits of information. One of the high-ranking aides, a man named Samuel Vargas, had begun to show signs of remorse and had offered clues to the identity of the hidden leader in exchange for a possible reduction of his sentence. Samuel mentioned one name in particular, an international businessman known as Viktor Ivanov, who had operated from the shadows and who, according to him, was the mastermind behind the network.

Lucas and Diana decided to focus on Viktor Ivanov, who had managed to stay under the radar throughout the investigation. With the information provided by Samuel Vargas, they began to gather evidence about Ivanov and his role in the laundering scheme. Further investigations revealed that Ivanov had a number of properties and companies in several countries, further complicating his location.

As they delved deeper into Viktor Ivanov's life and activities, they discovered that the businessman was linked to a number of legitimate financial operations covering his illicit activities. Ivanov used a network of contacts in the financial and business world to protect himself and divert any investigation in other directions.

Lucas and Diana faced a significant challenge in locating Ivanov. Their properties and businesses were spread out in strategic locations, and their ability to stay in the shadows complicated the task. However, the investigation had begun to show signs of progress when they identified a series of secret meetings that Ivanov attended at a luxurious mansion in Switzerland.

The team organized a covert operation to infiltrate the mansion and collect direct evidence about Ivanov's involvement in the laundering scheme. The operation required precise coordination and error-free execution, as any failure could alert Ivanov and allow him to escape.

During the operation, Lucas and Diana infiltrated the mansion and began searching for incriminating evidence. They found a hidden room containing documents and recordings of meetings detailing the operations of the laundering network and Ivanov's role in the scheme. The documents also included information about other international contacts and plans for future illegal operations.

While they were reviewing the documents, an unexpected confrontation with Ivanov's bodyguards ensued. The situation became dangerous, and Lucas and Diana had to act quickly to secure the evidence and avoid capture. The operation became a race against time to get out of the mansion with the essential information before reinforcements arrived.

With the evidence in hand, Lucas and Diana returned to their base of operations and began preparing a comprehensive report on Viktor Ivanov's role in the money laundering network. The information gathered not only confirmed Ivanov's involvement, but also revealed details about his international connections and his influence on the global scheme.

The public exposure of Viktor Ivanov and his laundering network became a high-impact media event. The media coverage and resulting legal action led to the arrest and prosecution of Ivanov and other key members of the network. The investigation had reached its climax, and the case was finally ready to be presented in court.

With the case closed and the laundering network dismantled, Lucas and Diana reflected on the work done and the impact it had had. They had faced significant challenges and managed to expose a global criminal network, but they knew that investigative work and the pursuit of justice did not end with a single case. The fight against organized crime and corruption would continue, and they were ready to face the next challenges with the same determination and courage.

Chapter 36: Echoes of the Past

With Viktor Ivanov arrested and the money laundering network dismantled, Lucas Ferrer and Diana Montero were in a moment of apparent calm. However, the resolution of the case brought with it new challenges and unexpected revelations. As the case prepared for court filing, echoes of the past began to emerge that threatened to further complicate the situation.

The team received an anonymous package at their office, which contained a video file and a letter with no return address. The video showed footage of a secret meeting between several individuals who were linked to the laundering network and discussing how to undo all the work done up to that point. The letter included an enigmatic message: "Not everything is resolved. The worst is yet to come."

Lucas and Diana decided to analyze the video and the letter carefully. The content of the video suggested that there were other elements of the laundering network that had not yet been discovered and that they were willing to take drastic measures to protect themselves. The letter's implicit threat seemed to confirm that all was not over.

Analysis of the video revealed a number of clues indicating that there was a possible leak of information within the investigation team or external partners involved in the case. The footage showed unknown people in contact with members of the laundering ring, suggesting there was a possible traitor in the ranks.

Diana decided to further investigate the connections and communications of the team and its associates. The suspicion of a possible internal leak generated great concern, as any compromised information could put the integrity of the investigation and the safety of everyone involved at risk.

While Diana reviewed communications and contacts, Lucas began researching the background of the anonymous package. He discovered that the package had been sent from a small post office in a nearby town, which provided a clue as to its origin. Analysis of the correspondence and fingerprints on the package revealed a possible link to a former TechNex Solutions employee who had gone missing shortly after the irregularities at the company were discovered.

Lucas and Diana decided to track down the missing former employee, who turned out to be a man named Ricardo Morales. With the help of contacts in the security sector, they managed to locate Ricardo in a secret shelter where he had been hiding due to the threats he had received from the laundering network.

Ricardo was willing to collaborate and provide insight into his experience at TechNex Solutions. He revealed that he had witnessed a number of secret meetings between members of the network and had been involved in the development of systems used to conceal illicit transactions. Ricardo also confirmed that he had received death threats to prevent him from speaking.

The information provided by Ricardo proved crucial to understanding how the laundering network had operated so effectively. He detailed how members of the network had manipulated technology systems to create a network of covert transfers and how they had used outside contacts to influence the investigation.

With Ricardo's testimony and the analysis of the video and letter, Lucas and Diana were faced with the task of identifying possible infiltrators in the investigation. Tension was rising as the team prepared to deal with any sabotage attempts and ensure that confidential information was protected.

The internal investigation revealed that one of the external consultants who had worked on the case had been in contact with the laundering network and had leaked information. This individual, who had been hired to help with data analysis, was linked to the network through his connections in the financial world.

With the traitor identified, Lucas and Diana worked with authorities to handle the situation and protect the integrity of the investigation. The exposure of the traitor and the adjustment of security measures ensured that the case moved forward without further interruption.

As the case neared its court filing, Lucas and Diana reflected on the additional complications they had faced. They had overcome significant challenges and found that the scope of the laundering scheme was even greater than initially imagined. The resolution of the case had become a triumph, but also a lesson in persistence and vigilance in the fight against organized crime.

Chapter 37: The Confrontation

With the traitor on the team identified and the money laundering case set to be presented in court, Lucas Ferrer and Diana Montero prepared for the last phase of the investigation. They knew that the trial would be a high-profile event, and that the forces at play were willing to do everything they could to avoid justice. The tension was palpable as they approached the final confrontation with those responsible.

Trial day arrived, and the courtroom was filled with press, lawyers, and observers. Media attention was focused on the case, which had become an international scandal due to the scale of the laundering network and high-profile connections involved. Lucas and Diana came forward as key witnesses, ready to present the evidence they had collected during the investigation.

The trial began with the presentation of evidence and witness testimony. The authorities and prosecutors in charge of the case offered a detailed account of how the laundering network had been dismantled, with solid evidence and corroborating testimonies. Lucas and Diana testified about the investigation process, key discoveries, and threats they had faced during the case.

During the trial, unexpected surprises arose. Defense lawyers for Viktor Ivanov and other defendants attempted to discredit witnesses and question the validity of the evidence presented. They argued that the evidence had been obtained in questionable ways and that it had been influenced by pressure from the media and public opinion.

At a critical moment in the trial, one of the defendants, Samuel Vargas, decided to cooperate with the defense and retract his previous testimony. This decision raised questions about the strength of the case and allowed defense attorneys to raise the possibility that the evidence was fabricated or tampered with.

Lucas and Diana faced a significant challenge in maintaining the credibility of their research. To counter the defense's arguments, they prepared a meticulous cross-examination and presented additional evidence confirming the authenticity of the evidence and testimony. The pressure was high, and the possibility of defendants evading justice was a constant concern.

As the trial progressed, an unexpected twist occurred. A key witness, a former TechNex Solutions employee who had been intimidated not to testify, appeared in court with additional evidence that further compromised the defendants. This witness, named Alejandro Rivas, had been in hiding for fear of reprisals, but decided to cooperate with the court after receiving adequate protection.

Alejandro's testimony provided crucial details about the network's covert operations and how the defendants had manipulated technology systems to conceal their activities. His statement supported the evidence presented by Lucas and Diana, and reinforced the strength of the case.

The trial reached its climax with the closing arguments of the lawyers. Prosecutors highlighted the magnitude of the laundering scheme and the overall impact it had had, while the defense sought to diminish the severity of the charges. The final verdict was in the hands of the jury, and the tension in the room was palpable.

Eventually, the jury reached a guilty verdict for Viktor Ivanov and several other key members of the laundering ring. The charges were confirmed and the evidence presented proved conclusive. The court's decision marked a significant triumph in the fight against organized crime and global corruption.

With the case closed and those responsible convicted, Lucas and Diana reflected on the journey they had gone through. They had faced formidable challenges, from threats and betrayals to tampering with evidence, but they had managed to achieve justice. The resolution of the case became a testament to the power of determination and integrity in the fight against crime.

The end of the trial also marked the beginning of a new stage in their lives. With the case solved, Lucas and Diana prepared to face new challenges and continue their work in investigation and justice. The global corruption ecosystem remained a complex battleground, but they were ready to confront it with the same courage and commitment they had shown throughout the case.

Chapter 38: The Last Game

With the verdict of the trial completed and most of those involved in the case convicted, Lucas Ferrer and Diana Montero thought that their work had come to an end. However, the recent resolution brought with it a series of unexpected events that would unleash a final wave of intrigue and danger.

A few days after the trial, Lucas received an anonymous call warning him that the case was not over. The voice on the line was distorted, but the message was clear: "The truth has not been told. There are still secrets to be discovered. Be ready for the last game." The call was abruptly interrupted, and the contact number could not be traced.

Intrigued and alarmed, Lucas and Diana decided to investigate the threat. They reviewed all documents and evidence in the case, looking for any hint of undisclosed information. During their review, they found a seemingly worthless document that had been overlooked in the mountain of evidence. This document, a handwritten note, appeared to be coded, and contained a series of numbers and enigmatic words.

Analysis of the document revealed a pattern that suggested the existence of a hidden message. Diana, with her skill in cryptography, worked to decipher the message. Eventually, he discovered that the document contained geographic coordinates and a specific date. The coordinates pointed to a remote location in the Swiss Alps, and the date was only a few days later.

Lucas and Diana decided to follow the trail and traveled to the indicated location. Upon arrival, they found an isolated cabin in the woods, apparently uninhabited. The hut was in ruins, but it appeared to have been used recently. Inside, they discovered a set of documents and files that had been hidden, including detailed records of additional operations and connections to even more powerful figures in the laundering network.

The documents revealed that Viktor Ivanov was not the only leader of the network. There was a secret council operating in the shadows that had planned a major move to bypass the authorities and continue laundering operations under a new scheme. The information also indicated that the members of this council were planning a series of transactions and financial movements to launder large sums of money in the global market.

Lucas and Diana understood that the threat in the anonymous call was real and that the case was not really closed. The existence of the secret council and its plans indicated that there was still an active corruption network that needed to be dismantled.

Determined to take on this new challenge, Lucas and Diana returned to the city to assemble the team and share the findings. The situation was dire, and they needed to act quickly to prevent the network from continuing to operate undetected.

As they prepared for a new phase of the investigation, they began to receive more anonymous threats, warning of the consequences of interfering with the council's plans. These threats increased the urgency and pressure on the team, which now had to operate under conditions of extreme caution and safety.

Lucas and Diana devised a plan to infiltrate the secret council's inner circle. Using the information and documents obtained, they managed to track the council's meetings and activities, and prepared for a series of covert operations. Every move had to be precisely calculated to prevent council members from escaping or destroying crucial evidence.

As they neared the climax of their investigation, Lucas and Diana were at the center of an operation that sought not only to dismantle a global criminal network, but also to protect themselves from a relentless enemy who was willing to do whatever it took to protect their interests.

The last phase of the case was shaping up to be the most dangerous and challenging. Lucas and Diana were ready to face the secret council and ensure that justice prevailed, not knowing that the greatest danger was yet to come.

Chapter 39: The Deadly Game

The air in the operating room was thick with tension. Lucas Ferrer and Diana Montero, along with their team, were prepared to carry out the riskiest mission of their careers. They had tracked the secret council to a luxurious mansion outside Geneva, Switzerland, that had become the center of their covert operations.

The mansion was surrounded by a series of high-tech security systems and a team of trained bodyguards. The entrance was heavily guarded and access was restricted, requiring meticulous planning to avoid detection. Lucas and Diana had devised an infiltration plan that included the use of false identities and advanced communication equipment.

The operation was carried out during a key board meeting, in which upcoming financial moves and schemes to divert large sums of money would be discussed. Lucas and Diana had infiltrated the mansion posing as security assistants and technology technicians. The meticulous preparation and use of sophisticated costumes allowed them to go unnoticed.

Once inside, the team moved quickly to install recording devices and obtain crucial evidence about the council's activities. The meeting room was filled with the council's most influential members, who discussed in detail illicit financial operations and plans to evade detection by authorities.

Lucas and Diana recorded the conversations and took note of important details. However, while they were in the room, they began to suspect that something was not right. The council members' conversation revolved around an escape plan and the removal of any incriminating evidence in case the undercover operation was discovered.

A few minutes later, Lucas and Diana's team realized that their presence had been detected. The security cameras, which had initially been disabled, were now up and running, and bodyguards began patrolling specific areas of the mansion. The council had anticipated possible infiltration and had taken extra precautions to protect itself.

The situation quickly became dangerous. Lucas and Diana ordered a quick evacuation, but found themselves trapped in a series of hallways and rooms in the mansion. The operation morphed into a race against time as they tried to find a safe exit and avoid being captured by bodyguards.

During their escape, they encountered Viktor Ivanov, who was present at the council meeting. Ivanov, who had been in a private conversation in a separate area, faced them with a cold and defiant expression. He had been aware of their infiltration and was preparing to confront them personally.

The confrontation with Ivanov was intense. Lucas and Diana, armed only with communication equipment and escape tools, had to use their wits and skills to outmaneuver Ivanov and his bodyguards. The confrontation was tense and dangerous, but they eventually managed to neutralize Ivanov and secure the exit from the mansion.

With the crucial evidence obtained and the confrontation with Ivanov resolved, Lucas and Diana managed to escape the mansion and return to their home base. The operation had been a success, but at a high cost. They had faced the impending danger and had managed to dismantle the secret council.

The team prepared a comprehensive report on the operation, including evidence obtained during the infiltration and confrontation with Ivanov. The evidence was turned over to the authorities and a series of additional legal actions were initiated against the council members and their associates.

The resolution of the case was an important triumph in the fight against organized crime and global corruption. Lucas and Diana reflected on the scale of the operation and the impact it had had on the money laundering network. The mission had proven to be definitive proof of his skill and determination in the pursuit of justice.

With the secret council dismantled and those responsible facing justice, Lucas and Diana prepared for the next phase of their career. The experience had been challenging and dangerous, but it had also strengthened his commitment to fighting crime.

Chapter 40: New Horizons

After weeks of intense operations and the outcome of the case, Lucas Ferrer and Diana Montero found themselves in a moment of reflection. The money laundering ring had been dismantled, the leaders of the secret council had been arrested, and the evidence gathered had led to a number of significant convictions. However, the case had left scars and unanswered questions.

Lucas and Diana met in his office, reviewing the latest documents related to the case. The battle had been won, but the war on crime and corruption continued. As they looked at the final reports and the results of the trial, they couldn't help but think about the impact their work had had on their lives and the world around them.

Lucas's phone rang. It was a call from a major international agency that was interested in offering him a position as a senior advisor for future global research. The offer was a recognition of his work in the recent case and his ability to handle complex situations. Lucas, with a mixture of enthusiasm and caution, considered the offer as a new opportunity to apply his experience on an even wider stage.

Diana, meanwhile, received a similar proposal to work at a non-governmental organization focused on fighting corruption and money laundering in developing countries. The offer promised him the opportunity to apply his knowledge in an international arena and contribute to the creation of effective policies to combat financial crime.

As they considered these new opportunities, they both reflected on the impact of their experiences. They had faced significant dangers, made personal and professional sacrifices, and had achieved resounding success. However, they had also learned about the limits and challenges of the system, and the constant need to adapt and evolve.

The conversation between Lucas and Diana veered into the future. They shared their expectations and fears about new opportunities, and how they could change the course of their lives and careers. They acknowledged that although the case was over, their commitment to justice and integrity would continue to guide their actions.

The last week of the case was also a moment of personal closure. Lucas and Diana said goodbye to their colleagues and the team that had worked tirelessly to solve the case. Celebrations were organized to recognize the effort and dedication of all those involved. Camaraderie and team spirit had been instrumental in overcoming obstacles and achieving success.

On the last day of their work at the office, Lucas and Diana sat on the balcony of their office, looking out over the city as the sun set. The view was beautiful, and the tranquility of the sunset contrasted with the intensity of recent events. They reflected on their experiences and how their lives had changed since the start of the case.

Lucas addressed Diana with a smile. "We have done a good job. But we also know that there will always be more challenges to face. What do you think if we continue with these new opportunities? There's a lot more to do, and I think we're ready to face whatever comes."

Diana nodded, a determined expression on her face. "I'm ready for anything. We have shown that we can face the impossible and move forward. Now is the time to move on and continue to make a difference."

With a sense of closure and anticipation, Lucas and Diana prepared for their new roles. The final chapter of their case had come to an end, but a new chapter in their lives was about to begin. The future was uncertain, but they were ready to face it with the same courage and commitment they had shown during the investigation.

As they said goodbye to the office and headed towards their new opportunities, the horizon stretched out before them, full of possibilities and challenges. The journey had been arduous, but each step had led to new understanding and strength. With the certainty that the work never ends and the determination to continue fighting for justice, Lucas and Diana entered a new chapter of their lives.

Did you love *Very Bad Momentum A gripping high-stakes Techno-thriller full of Conspiracy,Politics,Technology,Action and Espionage*? Then you should read *Unraveling Marriage, Unraveling Divorce A Domestic Thriller*[1] by Marcelo Palacios!

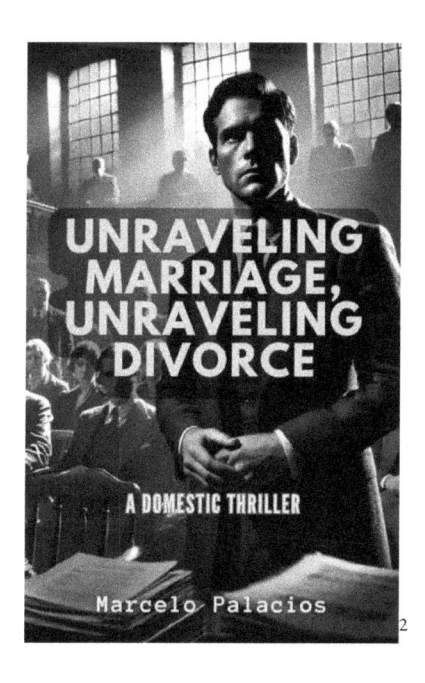

[2]

Thomas Pearson's life is about to unravel in ways he never saw coming. As a successful lawyer caught in a bitter divorce battle, he discovers that the woman he once trusted — his wife, Emma — has been playing a dangerous game, manipulating their marriage for years. As secrets begin to surface and betrayals unfold, Thomas must confront the web of lies, deceit, and manipulation that surrounds him.

In a high-stakes game of legal maneuvering and psychological warfare, Thomas fights for his freedom, but the stakes are higher than he ever imagined. With every step he takes, the truth becomes more elusive, and the people closest to him — including Emma, her powerful allies, and even his own allies — may not be who they appear to be.

---

1. https://books2read.com/u/mvVBXV

2. https://books2read.com/u/mvVBXV

"Unraveling Marriage, Unraveling Divorce" is a gripping psychological thriller and domestic suspense that delves into the complexities of trust, betrayal, and the hidden truths that lurk beneath the surface of even the most intimate relationships. With everything on the line, Thomas must decide how far he's willing to go to expose the truth, even if it means losing everything.

Will he unravel the conspiracy before it's too late? Or will he fall victim to the manipulation that's been set in motion against him? The clock is ticking.

Prepare for a shocking journey through lies, power, and a battle for survival in the darkest corners of the human psyche.

Also by Marcelo Palacios

El Club de los Pecados Un Thriller Psicológico
La Habitación Resonante Un Thriller Psicológico
Mentiras en Código Un Thriller Político
The Political Lies A Political Thriller
Sin's Fraternity A Psychological Thriller
El Cuarto de los Ecos Un Thriller Psicologico lleno de Suspenso
The Room of Echoes A Psychological Thriller Full of Suspense
El Espejo Perturbador Un Thriller Psicologico
The Disturbing Mirror A Psychological Thriller
Luces Apagadas en la Ciudad Brillante Un Thriller Psicológico,Crimen y Policial
Lights Out in the Shining City A Psychological, Crime and Police Thriller
Under the Cloak of Horror A Criminal Psychological Thriller full of Abuse, Corruption, Mystery, Suspense and Adventure
The Housemaid's Shadow A Psychological Thriller
Unraveling Marriage, Unraveling Divorce A Domestic Thriller
Broadband Horizons : A Technothriller Cyberpunk-Steampunk Novel
Mindstorm Protocol Expansion : A Post-Apocalyptic, Dystopian and Technological Thriller Science Fiction Novel
The Power of Invisible Chains : A Conspiracy, Crime & Political Thriller
The Watcher's Silent Crusade : A Police Procedurals & Crime Thriller
Very Bad Momentum A gripping high-stakes Techno-thriller full of Conspiracy,Politics,Technology,Action and Espionage

Milton Keynes UK
Ingram Content Group UK Ltd.
UKHW042002291124
451915UK00004B/378